House *of* Decadence

House *of* Decadence

MARINA ANDERSON

sphere

SPHERE

First published in Great Britain in 1995 by X Libris
This paperback edition published in 2012 by Sphere

A CIP catalogue record for this book
is available from the British Library.

ISBN 978-0-7515-5169-3

Typeset in Sabon by M Rules
Printed and bound in Great Britain by
Clays Ltd, St Ives plc

Papers used by Sphere are from well-managed forests
and other responsible sources.

MIX
Paper from
responsible sources
FSC
www.fsc.org   FSC® C104740

Sphere
An imprint of
Little, Brown Book Group
100 Victoria Embankment
London EC4Y 0DY

An Hachette UK Company
www.hachette.co.uk

www.littlebrown.co.uk

House *of* Decadence

Chapter One

The room was dark, the heavy drapes drawn across the windows to block out the summer sun. At the far end of the room, standing on a raised platform, was a tall, slender young woman, her beautiful face framed by a mane of tawny hair. She was completely naked, her small breasts swollen, the nipples tight with arousal.

It was silent in the room, but it was a silence charged with an electric air of eroticism. Seated in the comfort of their leather chairs, three men and a woman watched the tawny-haired beauty as, following an instruction from one of them, she parted her long legs and began to move her fingers between her thighs. Her breathing became more audible as her excitement grew and her body began to tremble. Her large, violet eyes, for which she was famous, widened as her thighs shook with an approaching orgasm. Almost imperceptibly she changed the rhythm of her fingers and some of the tension was released from her body.

'You're cheating, Alessandra,' said a deep voice from the darkness of the room. 'You know how much I hate it when you cheat.'

Immediately the girl's fingers quickened and soon her back was arching, and her breasts thrust forward as she approached the point of no return.

'How many orgasms will this be?' Leonora Balocchi asked her brother, Fabrizio, quietly.

'Five.'

'And she was only allowed four?'

'That's right.'

'Which means she'll be punished for this one?' There was no mistaking the pleasure in Leonora's voice.

'Naturally. A fact of which Alessandra is clearly very aware,' he responded. 'That's why she tried to cheat.'

There was a small gasp from the girl on the platform and immediately Fabrizio and his sister stopped speaking, concentrating all their attention on Alessandra instead. She struggled desperately to delay her pleasure, but as her fingers continued to stimulate the highly responsive damp flesh between her thighs it proved impossible, and with a tiny cry of despair she climaxed, her body shaking from head to foot.

The four other people in the room remained silent, but now their breathing was audible as they waited for Fabrizio to decide on his lover's punishment.

Getting to his feet he stepped up onto the platform. Although he was six foot one, Alessandra was only a couple of inches shorter than him, and he rested a hand lightly on her shoulder. 'One too many, I'm afraid.'

Alessandra didn't reply, but he could feel her body shaking beneath his touch.

'You still have twenty minutes left to go,' he continued smoothly. 'Your first punishment will be an easy one. It's time for you to have the blindfold on.'

Alessandra stiffened, drawing away from her lover's hand, but she didn't protest. Instead, she lowered her head with an air of resigned submission. She hated the blindfold, as Fabrizio knew very well, which was why he'd chosen it. So many things had happened to her in the darkness brought by the black velvet band that her fear of it was nearly as great as the incredible pleasure she'd received; bizarre, pain-filled pleasure that had possessed her during the long, strange sexual sessions of initiation into the world of Fabrizio and the other three watchers in the room.

Fabrizio drew the black band from his pocket, fastened it over her eyes and ran a finger down her spine, scratching the skin with his fingernail as he did so. 'You look ravishing,' he murmured. 'I wonder if you have any idea how much pleasure this gives me.'

Alessandra didn't answer him. Now she stood, unable to see anything at all, and waited for someone to come and start arousing her once again, determined to give her yet another forbidden orgasm which would lead to further punishment. Yet despite her fear she was excited, because her body had learnt to enjoy the dark pleasures. Sometimes she wondered how far Fabrizio would take her, and if she would ever choose to refuse him.

Fabrizio left the platform and as he returned to his seat touched Leonora on the knee. 'You may try and bring her to orgasm now,' he said casually.

Leonora hurried to the platform. This was what she loved, to be in control, whether of a man or a woman, dominating and forcing sexual pleasure from them against their will. She was as big a control freak as her brother but less subtle in her methods. At five foot four she was much shorter than the other woman, but it didn't matter because she immediately turned Alessandra's body slightly, angling it so that as she knelt between the girl's legs, the three men seated below the platform would have the best view possible. As her hands circled Alessandra's ankles and began to slide upwards, massaging the calves as they went, Alessandra tried to move back, to remove herself from the insidiously arousing caresses that she knew were coming. Leonora gripped the other woman's legs tightly, and as her hands stroked the insides of Alessandra's thighs, Alessandra began to moan with despair. Now Leonora's fingers were parting the girl's sex lips and she held her mouth close to the exposed vulva, breathing softly against it so that Alessandra knew only too well what was going to happen to her.

The anticipation added to Alessandra's excitement and once more her nipples formed tight little peaks and the skin rippled over the surface of her flat belly. After several seconds of almost unbearable tension Leonora's tongue struck with incredible precision, swirling around Alessandra's already swollen clitoris so that her victim's moans of mingled distress and pleasure increased in volume. Leonora could feel her silk panties becoming damp with her own excitement as Alessandra fought once more to prevent the forbidden pleasure from overcoming her. As she licked, sweat formed on her top lip and on her breasts.

'No! No!' Alessandra cried.

'Be silent,' Fabrizio called, and Leonora chose that moment to draw the tight little nub of flesh into her mouth, sucking hard on it. She could imagine the delicious sensations that must be suffusing Alessandra's belly and, all at once, while continuing to suck on the centre of Alessandra's pleasure, she roughly pushed three fingers inside the other woman, moving them in and out in a fierce, rapid rhythm.

Within seconds Alessandra threw her head back and the tendons of her neck stood out like whipcords as sexual tension caused every muscle within her to tighten until, with a scream, she succumbed to yet another orgasm of unbearably intense pleasure.

'You lack control still,' said Leonora, standing up in front of the girl. Although she knew that she should now leave the platform, Alessandra's breasts proved too much of a temptation, and reaching out Leonora pinched each of the nipples hard between her fingers. To everyone's amazement Alessandra's body was convulsed with another spasm of pleasure.

'Does that merit two punishments?' asked Leonora brightly, as she returned to her seat.

Fabrizio didn't answer his sister. He was watching his lover through narrowed eyes. Her beautiful hair, usually so immaculately groomed, was a tangled mess, the roots drenched with sweat. Her cheeks were flushed, as were her chest and her breasts. She looked wonderfully debased and humiliated and his erection inside his trousers was painfully hard. Despite this he had no intention of pleasuring himself until much later in the day. This was entertainment, and yet another experience for Alessandra. Looking over to his left he nodded to Renato Staffieri, his best friend and Leonora's lover. It was Renato's turn to punish Alessandra, a fact which amused Fabrizio because he knew that this really wasn't Renato's scene. His sexuality, although intense and wide-ranging, was of a different nature from Fabrizio's, but he enjoyed all the games and had never yet let Fabrizio down.

Renato walked quietly to the platform, pausing only to collect something from a small table as he went.

Once on the platform he pulled Alessandra's hands behind her back and quickly fastened them with a pair of leather handcuffs. Next he pushed her to her knees, but she knelt too far down and he tugged on her hair until she was kneeling upright in the position he wanted. Alessandra uttered a tiny cry of pain but Fabrizio could see that she was, if anything, even more excited now than earlier in the game and he smiled to himself.

It was clear that she assumed this to be her full punishment, but Renato had correctly guessed that because she'd climaxed twice she could be punished twice. He moved away from the kneeling girl, who stared sightlessly out into the room, and at the last moment, just before stepping down from the platform, he turned, and with a quick flick of his right wrist struck Alessandra a glancing blow across her swollen breasts with a latex whip. Alessandra screamed in shock and Fabrizio watched her closely as Renato returned to his seat.

A tiny tear rolled from beneath the blindfold and Fabrizio started to rise to his feet, but then he saw how hard Alessandra's nipples were, and saw too the moisture running down the insides of her thighs and he knew then that her pleasure was far outweighing her distress. 'You only have another five minutes to go,' he called out. 'I'm sure you can avoid further punishment in that time.'

Alessandra moved her head around, trying to see something out of the corners of the blindfold, but he knew that she wouldn't be successful. He was aware that Franco Pierotti, his private secretary and frequent companion, was expecting to try to bring Alessandra to another orgasm in the final five minutes but decided against it. He himself would be the one to exert the ultimate power, to wrench yet more pleasure from the humiliated girl and then allow Franco to punish her. Knowing Alessandra's body as well as he did it was hardly likely that he would fail.

With three long strides he was quickly on the platform, removing the handcuffs before pushing her onto her back. Then he knelt beside her prone body, running a hand briefly over her breasts, cupping the soft flesh before moving his hands lower and starting to massage her belly in the round circular movements that she loved so much. She whimpered with rising desire, and despite the fact that she was trying not to climax, her hips began to lift off the floor in order to increase the pleasure he was giving her.

'Be very careful,' he cautioned her. 'You may not like the final punishment.'

Immediately she stopped moving but Fabrizio's expertise was so great that it made no difference; even motionless she would be helpless to resist the pleasure he was going to give her, a very special pleasure that he'd taught her to enjoy. Carefully he pressed the heel of his hand hard against the bottom of her belly causing pressure to increase in her bladder, which added extra stimulation to all the nerve endings in her engorged pelvic area. She uttered a gurgling sound of protest which he ignored, and as he continued to press with the heel of his left hand, his right hand moved between her soaking thighs until he located the clitoris which was half retracted.

He teased it lightly with his fingers until it swelled and emerged from its protective hood once more. Now his fingers closed around it and he heard Alessandra's breath catch in her throat as he started to apply gentle pressure, pressure that he gradually increased until she was moaning with discomfort, but it was a discomfort that always led to a shattering pleasure-pain that sent her into paroxysms of ecstasy.

He looked down at her long, lean body with the tiny breasts and beautiful olive skin and suddenly he couldn't wait any longer. The fingers of his right hand pinched hard on the stem of her clitoris, while at the same time he pushed deeper into her belly. Her desperately over-stimulated nerve endings, unable to withstand it any longer, exploded into an orgasm of such intensity that Alessandra's body jerked up off the floor and she screamed in horrified pleasure as her arms and legs spasmed and jerked uncontrollably.

Fabrizio leant over her and kissed her full on the mouth. 'You're so beautiful,' he whispered against her ear. 'So beautiful and so shameless. It's a pity that you have to be punished, but that's the game.'

Striding down from the platform he signalled for Franco to administer the final punishment, whispering into his secretary's ear exactly what he wanted him to do. He had something else on his mind as well now, and even as his sobbing mistress was pulled to her feet and forced to bend forward from the waist so that Franco could thrust himself deep inside the tight, forbidden entrance between the cheeks of her bottom, he was leaving the room. He had to be sure that the advertisement was in the magazine.

The last thing he heard was her sharp cry of pain, pain that he could imagine only too well, but that he also knew would lead to a primeval pleasure that as yet Alessandra was ashamed to enjoy. It was, as Fabrizio knew, a very special kind of pain.

Chapter Two

Megan Stewart flinched as the pain of her throbbing tooth increased. She wondered if there was anything worse than really bad toothache, and glancing at the library clock saw that there were still three hours to go before her dental appointment.

'Hurting a lot?' asked Alice, her fellow library assistant.

Megan nodded. 'I'm not very brave when it comes to pain,' she confessed.

'Who is?'

Their conversation was interrupted by an angry, middle-aged man. 'I've been looking for *How Did She Die?* for half an hour now,' he said furiously.

'According to the lady I asked when I got here, the book's meant to be in, but it's clearly been put back in the wrong section.'

Megan plastered a smile on her aching face and set off to search the library shelves. She eventually found the book in the family saga section.

'There, what did I tell you?' asked the man, satisfaction and annoyance mingling in his voice. 'Pure carelessness, that's what it is, pure carelessness.'

'I'm very sorry,' said Megan. 'I can't think how it happened.'

'Can't think more likely,' snapped the man, grabbing the book and marching off to the desk.

Megan felt like weeping. It was always difficult dealing with the public, particularly on a hot summer's day at the beginning of the school holidays when the place was crowded with noisy children accompanied by their irritable mothers, and fraught pensioners who were used to a more tranquil atmosphere. However, with the persistent throbbing pain in her left cheek the day was proving even more difficult than usual.

At two o'clock, when she was finally sitting in the relative peace of the dentist's waiting room, she tried to distract herself from the thought of what lay ahead. Her fear of the dentist was so great that she never went for regular check-ups which was, she realised, why she'd ended up in this situation. It was obvious that the dentist was running late and she tried to concentrate on the forthcoming weekend. Unfortunately it didn't hold anything very exciting. It would be the usual Saturday night at the pub with Nick and his group of friends, where she'd have to listen to them talking about football, before she and Nick went back to her flat for twenty minutes of sex, after which Nick would snore all night. On Sunday morning they'd probably have sex again, and then Nick would talk at great length about his work selling fitted kitchens. It was hardly a weekend to distract her from the thought of the dentist's drill.

'There must be more to life than this,' muttered Megan.

'Excuse me?' asked a woman sitting next to her.

'I'm sorry, I was just thinking out loud,' explained Megan. The pain in her cheek stabbed viciously and she rested the palm of her hand against it to try and ease the discomfort. The woman moved away slightly, as though worried that Megan was unhinged.

Feeling utterly depressed Megan picked up a newspaper from the table in the middle of the room. On a sudden whim she turned to the job adverts page, deciding that it would be interesting to see what exciting opportunities there were for dissatisfied girls of twenty-three like herself. Not that she'd ever change her job, she'd probably never even leave Lincolnshire, but at least it might take her mind off the pain.

She was surprised at how many people needed companions, either for themselves or for elderly relatives, a job which she imagined would be even more depressing than her current one. She was about to turn to another page when her eye was caught by a boxed advert which was far more to her liking.

Help urgently needed to catalogue and organise extensive library of rare books and first editions in the heart of the Sussex countryside. Good salary and excellent live-in accommodation provided. Apply in writing to Box No. 6724 giving qualifications and references. Duration of employment approximately 6 months.

'Miss Stewart,' called the dental nurse. Megan's stomach lurched, and as she got to her feet she grabbed the paper and shoved it into her shopping bag. The post had probably already been filled, she thought to herself, but she could check when she got home. It was just that compared with the chaos in the library that morning, the peace and tranquillity of the Sussex countryside sounded very alluring.

Twenty minutes later she emerged from the dentist, her mouth frozen and pain-free. But instead of returning to the library she went back to her flat, ringing in to say that she felt too unwell to work, before settling down to re-read the advert. She couldn't understand why it held such an attraction for her. It wasn't as though she'd really been considering changing her job, but for some reason she felt that she'd been meant to read it, and meant to follow it up.

The paper turned out to be only a few days old, confirming her feeling that she was intended to apply. She knew that if she discussed it with Nick he wouldn't want her to. They'd been going out for nearly a year now and it was a very comfortable arrangement for him. The trouble was, it was no longer enough for Megan, and she knew that if she didn't break out of her safe rut soon, it would be too late. Within another six months Nick would probably propose and she, out of lethargy and fear of being left on the shelf, would accept. In another two years she'd be married and probably a mother. 'But I won't have lived,' she said aloud. 'I ought to do more while I'm still young.'

Finally she wrote a letter of application, but then panicked. It was only after ringing her best friend, Kathy, who was full of enthusiasm for the plan, that she actually found the courage to post it that same night.

She didn't mention what she'd done to anyone else, and as several days passed she decided that this was fortunate because she clearly wasn't going to hear anything about it. Then, exactly a week later, she was asked to an interview.

'What should I wear?' she asked Kathy when they met for a drink after work.

Kathy shrugged. 'Nothing too threatening,' she advised. 'You know what these moneyed families who live in country houses are like. Sensible shoes and a light brown skirt, preferably well below the knee, are the sort of thing they appreciate.'

'I suppose so,' agreed Megan. 'Mind you, that doesn't sound much more exciting than working in a public library.'

'At least you'll get a chance to meet new people,' Kathy pointed out. 'Besides, there might be a handsome son who works in the City and falls madly in love with you during a visit home one weekend.'

'He's not going to fall madly in love with me if I'm wearing sensible shoes and an ankle-length brown skirt, is he?' retorted Megan.

Kathy laughed. 'You'll have to do the classic librarian's trick. Pile all that long curly hair of yours up on top of your head and put on a pair of horn-rimmed glasses while you're working. Then, when the son arrives, whip off the glasses, pull out the hair pins, shake your head and hey-presto, you're the gorgeous Renaissance-style heroine that he's always longed for.'

'You're laughing at me aren't you?' said Megan. 'You don't really think this is going to make any difference to my life.'

'I do!' protested Kathy. 'I think it's going to make a big difference. For a start it will stop you drifting into an engagement with Nick, which would be an absolute disaster. The pair of you haven't got anything in common, except sex.'

'And even that's not what it was,' confessed Megan.

'Well there you are then. What have you got to lose? Go for it girl.'

'I haven't told Nick,' confessed Megan.

'Why should you? You haven't been offered the job yet. Time enough to worry about that if you turn out to be the successful candidate. Look, I've got to dash. I've met this gorgeous hunk at the office and we're going out for a meal later. When's the interview?'

'Monday.'

'Well, give me a ring when you get back, tell me all about it.'

'OK,' agreed Megan. 'And you really think I should wear sensible shoes?' she added.

'Definitely,' said Kathy firmly. 'Nobody wears stiletto heels when cataloguing books in the heart of the Sussex countryside! Good luck.'

In her imagination Megan had been picturing a slightly above average-sized country house, with the usual air of genteel poverty and slight decay, so when she parked her red Peugeot in front of the double garage and stepped out to look about her she could hardly believe her eyes.

The house was an enormous Victorian mansion built,

she guessed, around 1870 and set in what appeared to be at least twenty acres of ground. Furthermore, there was no sign of poverty, neglect or decay. The lawns, as far as she could see, were in immaculate condition, as were the flower beds. The driveway, which was crazy-paved, didn't have a single weed on it, and every window in the house sparkled in the sunlight, while the paintwork looked so fresh it could have been done that very week. Nerves overwhelmed her and her breathing felt constricted as she rang the front door bell.

A middle-aged maid let her in, took her name and then hurried away, after indicating that Megan should take a seat on one of the tapestry-cushioned, ladder-backed chairs that stood against the wall.

The hall was enormous, the walls decorated with the most incredible paintings, and everywhere there were small tables holding beautiful, fragile ornaments that looked so valuable Megan was terrified she might break something even before the interview began.

She had to wait a good ten minutes, which only increased her nervousness. When she finally heard the sound of a door opening at the far end of the hall she felt a flutter in her chest, a flutter which only increased when she set eyes on her prospective employer for the first time. She'd been expecting to meet an elderly member of the minor British aristocracy, and the sight of this tall, dark-haired man with his high cheekbones, heavily-lidded eyes and wide, sensual mouth came as a terrible shock. He was comparatively young too, not much more than thirty she guessed, and impeccably dressed. His dark blue suit was obviously tailor-made, and his crisp white shirt looked as though he'd taken it out of its box that very morning. The pale blue and yellow tie with matching handkerchief in the pocket of his jacket also looked new, and Megan wondered if she'd come to the right place. This man didn't look as though he'd be in the least bit interested in rare books and first editions. He looked more like a high-powered businessman, or even a film star, and he most certainly didn't look English.

He held out his hand. 'I trust you had a pleasant journey, Miss Stewart?'

'It was fine,' she assured him hastily. 'Your directions were very good.'

He nodded. 'Naturally. I'm a man who knows how to organise things, but unfortunately I do not have the time to cover everything. That is why I have advertised for assistance. Please, follow me. I'm sure you would like a coffee after your long drive and we will talk together in the library. That way you'll be able to see for yourself what kind of task you would be undertaking, should I decide to offer you the position.'

With one final, slightly amused glance at her the man turned and began to walk briskly down the hallway, Megan following behind him. She was horribly conscious of how dowdy she was looking and silently cursed Kathy and the sensible shoes and skirt that she was wearing. But then how could she have known what to expect? This wasn't the kind of man you expected to place an advert in *Country Life*. She was certainly suitably dressed to meet with an elderly scholar's approval; unfortunately this man wasn't an elderly scholar.

The library was also large, but unlike the hall it was in a horrible mess. Books lay everywhere in chaotic heaps, and although she didn't like to stare Megan was sure that she saw a first edition of *Alice in Wonderland* lying on top of one of the piles.

'As you can see, this will be quite a task for whoever takes it on,' said the dark-haired man.

Megan nodded. 'Did someone leave halfway through getting it organised?'

He shook his head. 'Not at all. Let me explain. First

of all I've been remiss in not introducing myself. My name is Fabrizio Balocchi. My sister and I recently inherited this house from our bachelor uncle. He lived here for the last thirty years of his life, building up a catering business for the rich and famous people of this country. We also inherited this catering firm, but as we already have our own family business in Tuscany I cannot spare more than six months to get my uncle's affairs straight here.'

'I see,' said Megan, realising that she'd been right. The books meant little to a man who was probably nothing more than a playboy and a complete philistine.

'Tell me about the work you do at the moment,' said Fabrizio.

Megan explained exactly what working in the library entailed, including dealing with truculent members of the British public. He watched her thoughtfully, never smiling but looking so intently at her that she felt distinctly uncomfortable. It was as though he was trying to see into her soul, and she wondered if he was afraid that she was under-qualified for the job, or perhaps would vanish after a few days taking some of the valuable first editions with her. Finally she ran out of things to say and fell silent.

'Your work does not sound very interesting,' he said. His voice was neutral, as though it was of no consequence to him whether it was or it wasn't.

'I enjoyed it at first,' said Megan. 'Now I feel it's time for a change.'

For the first time his face showed some expression. His eyes looked brighter and he put his head on one side as he looked thoughtfully at her. 'So you wish for your life to change?'

'Yes, I suppose so.'

'You suppose or you know?'

Megan felt flustered. 'I know that I want a change. I suppose I hadn't thought of it as life-altering, that's all.'

'But of course your life would alter. For a start you would live here, in this house. You would be living with me and my companions. We would like you to feel like one of the family, but this would be difficult if you have already left a family behind. You haven't mentioned whether or not you have a boyfriend.'

Megan stared at him. 'I didn't think it was important.'

'Yes, it's important. If I employ you I don't wish you to become homesick, or ask for every weekend off in order to see your partner.'

'But you wouldn't expect me to work seven days a week?'

'You would get one weekend off in three,' he said shortly. 'Is that a problem?'

Megan shook her head. 'No. And as a matter of fact I do have a boyfriend but we don't live together or anything like that.' She couldn't imagine why she was telling the Italian so much about herself, except for the fact that he clearly wanted to know and she sensed that if she wasn't perfectly honest with him she stood no chance of getting the job.

'So this boyfriend is more a friend than a lover, is that what you're saying?' He kept his eyes fixed on her face as he waited for her reply.

Megan shifted uncomfortably from one foot to the other. 'Well, I wouldn't say that exactly but ... '

'It is of no importance. I understand very well what you're trying to say. You would not miss your friends in Lincolnshire if you were to live here for six months?'

'Well, it's not as though I'm taking a job in Australia is it?' said Megan with a smile. 'I can easily drive up to see them.'

'I shall need you here for a lot of the time. Also, I do

not like having strangers in my house. I would not wish you to bring your friends here.'

'The idea never crossed my mind,' said Megan truthfully.

'Have you ever been affianced?' he asked abruptly.

Megan was beginning to feel very uncomfortable indeed under this intense personal questioning. 'I've never been engaged, no.'

'So, unlike many of your contemporaries, you are not in a rush to be married?'

'I want to live a little more before I settle down,' explained Megan.

'Ah!' His eyes lit up. 'This I can understand, and of this I approve. I too believe it is important to live life to the full.'

'The problem is,' said Megan, 'that working with books is quite a solitary occupation. I suppose if I really wanted to live life to the full I'd emigrate to the States, wouldn't I?'

'Not at all. Already you have answered an advertisement which gives you the opportunity to live in a different part of your country and to meet new people. I can assure you that if you take this job you will most certainly learn to live life to the full. We

Italians understand how to do this, perhaps rather better than the English.'

Megan wanted to defend her fellow countrymen but since she'd never met anyone like this man in her life, and as she was already feeling more alive talking to him than she'd ever felt before, there wasn't very much she could say. 'I think I could do a very good job here,' she assured him. 'I do know a lot about books and, like you, I'm good at organising. I presume you want everything catalogued?'

Fabrizio didn't answer. In fact, to her dismay Megan realised that he no longer appeared to be listening to her, but instead had turned away and was pulling on a bell-rope, presumably in order to have her shown out.

'You've probably already decided how you'd like them catalogued,' she continued, talking far too fast because all at once she knew that she desperately wanted this job. She wanted a chance to see more of this incredibly attractive, dark-haired man who, although he frightened her for reasons she didn't understand, also intrigued her.

'I'm sorry?' He looked vaguely at her.

'I was saying . . . '

At that moment the library door opened and a girl of around Megan's own age walked in. She was of average height, and had dark eyes that were so much like Fabrizio's that Megan realised she must be his sister. However, whereas his hair was dark, hers was a beautiful shade of honey-blonde, and her voluptuous figure was set off to perfection by the riding outfit she was wearing. She smiled at Megan, tapping her riding crop against the side of her long boots. Confronted with such beauty, Megan felt even worse about herself.

'You're the librarian who's come from Lincolnshire, aren't you?' asked the girl.

'Let me introduce you,' said Fabrizio swiftly. 'Leonora, this is Miss Megan Stewart. Miss Stewart, this is my sister Leonora. Leonora knows nothing about books; she is far more interested in her horses.'

Leonora smiled at Megan in a friendly fashion. 'I do read books, but not ones like these. I prefer novels about love and desire. Tell me Megan, what kind of books do you like to read?'

'Biographies mainly,' confessed Megan. Then, realising that this sounded very stuffy she added, 'There's often a lot of passion in them. It's amazing what kind of love-lives people led in the olden days.'

'Indeed?' asked Fabrizio. 'You think that people were more licentious then than now?'

'I wouldn't say licentious,' murmured Megan. 'It's just that they weren't like we imagine them to have been.'

'Not like *you* imagine them to have been perhaps,' said Fabrizio, glancing at his sister.

'Well, it's been a pleasure to meet you,' said Leonora, holding out her hand. 'I do hope that we meet again.' As she turned on her heel to leave the room, Megan saw her give her brother an almost imperceptible nod.

After she'd left there was a short silence and then Fabrizio pulled out a chair for Megan and sat down at the table opposite her. 'I would like to offer you the job,' he said abruptly.

Megan stared at him in astonishment. 'But you haven't even asked for references.'

'I trust my own judgement. However, I do have a contract for you to sign, a contract in which you agree to stay until the work is completed unless I myself break the terms and conditions. We wish you to become part of our whole way of life here, do you understand me?'

He stared at her. Megan's skin prickled and to her

astonishment her nipples hardened and she felt them brushing against her blouse. She couldn't understand what was happening to her, but there was something about the way he was looking at her, and something dark and unsettling about his insistence on her entering into the family's way of life that was both erotic and unnerving.

'I'm very flattered,' she said at last. 'I'd be delighted to take the contract away, and then as long as we both feel we suit each other ...'

Fabrizio's face darkened. 'Clearly I haven't made myself plain. I wish you to sign the contract here, before you leave.'

'I don't understand,' said Megan. 'You can't expect me to make up my mind this quickly.'

Fabrizio sighed. 'Very well, you may take it away if you wish, but naturally I cannot guarantee that in the meantime I may not interview someone even better qualified than you. Then you would lose out on this opportunity. If you accept the position now, I shall not interview any other candidates.'

'Perhaps if I could have a few more details,' said Megan, who certainly didn't want to lose her chance of getting the job.

The Italian rose to his feet. 'Certainly. Let's begin by having a tour of the house. Come with me.' Without even glancing behind to see if she was following, he walked swiftly out of the library, along the hall and into what she assumed must be the main drawing room. Once again she was taken by surprise. There was no faded, antique furniture here, simply beautiful, tasteful chairs and a vast, deep sofa, all in cream. The room was light and airy, but the paintings on the walls were of a very different kind and she looked in surprise at one of them.

'That's Titian's *Doge Andrea Gritti*, isn't it?' she asked, looking at the glorious red and gold of the Doge's clothing.

Fabrizio looked surprised. 'You recognise it?'

'Of course. I love Titian's work.'

'Then you will like the one on the first landing, *La Bella*. I too greatly admire his work and *La Bella* fascinates me. The woman is so enigmatic. There is much that is hidden in her eyes. It is far more exciting for men if they feel that women are keeping part of themselves secret. There is excitement in attempting to discover such secrets.'

Megan felt that this was a most peculiar conversation

for them to be having, and also a rather unsettling one. 'I suppose so,' she murmured.

'This is the room where we usually gather in the evenings,' he explained. 'Come, now I will take you upstairs and show you the room that will be yours if you accept the post.'

In order to reach it they had to go up two flights of stairs. On the first landing Fabrizio pointed to the Titian painting that he'd mentioned earlier. 'Do you understand what I mean about her expression?' he asked.

Megan stared at the woman and after a few minutes she thought that she did understand what he meant. The woman might well have had secrets. There was a hint of amusement in the superficially bland face, but you had to look very hard to see it. 'It's wonderful,' she agreed.

To her surprise Fabrizio laughed. 'The painting or her expression?'

'The painting.'

'Her expression troubles you doesn't it?'

'No. Why should it?'

'A question I ask myself,' he murmured. 'Now, let us find your room.'

He appeared to be assuming that she would take the position. And in truth, the more she saw of the house, and her employer, the more desperate she was to stay here, but she was still worried by the fact that he wanted her to sign an agreement before leaving. It seemed so strange and unprofessional, particularly for a man who was beginning to show himself as experienced in employing people and taking decisions. Her earlier opinion of him as a philistine had been hastily reversed.

On the next floor, which was all luxuriously carpeted, he opened the door to a bedroom at least three times the size of her own flat. She couldn't help but utter a tiny cry of delight; it was so beautiful. The walls and fabrics were all a glorious shade of dusky pink, and the bed was enormous with a long fringed cover and a high, soft padded headboard above which, suspended just below the ceiling, hung matching drapes. There were spotlights around the room, reproduction Italian prints on the walls, tiny but beautifully made stools, and chests of drawers with marble tops.

'Through here is an en-suite bathroom,' explained Fabrizio, opening a door that had been concealed by a hanging curtain. 'Be careful, there are two steps down.'

Megan walked into the bathroom, took one look at the sunken bath and the mirrors on three of the walls, the gold taps and the glass jars containing various perfumes and bath salts, and hurried back into the bedroom. Such luxury for an employee seemed incredible. It was as though the room was a baited trap, but it was a trap that she was becoming more and more anxious to walk into.

'I hope it is satisfactory?' queried Fabrizio as she stared around the bedroom once more.

'It's out of this world,' confessed Megan.

'Good. What were you expecting? A small room in the attic?'

Megan laughed. 'Hardly, but the idea of luxury like this had never crossed my mind.'

'I believe that everyone should have the opportunity to experience luxury, and to learn to use their senses to the full,' he said enigmatically. 'Now, we will return to the library and discuss the financial terms.'

On their way downstairs Megan began to feel a little nervous. It was all too good to be true, and Fabrizio was far too anxious to get her to take the job. Despite his attempts at indifference she knew that he wanted her to work for him, and she found it hard to believe that it was simply her abilities as a librarian that made her so indispensable. On the other hand, it was hard to believe that she was of any interest to him as a person in her own right.

She had no illusions about herself. She was attractive enough, with a good figure, and her naturally curly, long dark brown hair gave her a Renaissance-style look, but she wasn't in the least sophisticated. In fact, because she was lacking in self-confidence she never dressed to show her figure off to its best advantage. She didn't doubt for one moment that Fabrizio Balocchi was used to a very different type of woman. Just the same, there had to be a reason for him wanting her so badly, and it was possible that the reason was a dangerous one.

It would be foolish, she thought, to commit herself to staying here, cut off from friends and family, only to find herself in a difficult situation from which she couldn't escape. Her fears increased as she saw another man coming up the stairs towards her. He was around the same height as Fabrizio but his face was far softer. He had a mop of dark brown curly hair and as he drew level he gave her a gentle smile.

'You must be Miss Stewart?' Megan nodded and

held out her hand. 'It's a pleasure to meet you,' he continued. 'I do hope that Fabrizio hasn't frightened you off. The library is in a terrible mess, but although he may seem like a hard task-master he wouldn't expect you to put it to rights in less than six months, would you Fabrizio?'

Megan glanced over her shoulder to where the Italian was standing behind her. He looked consideringly at the other man and then shook his head.

'Of course not. But I'm sure that I haven't alarmed Miss Stewart. Miss Stewart, this is Renato Staffieri, my sister's boyfriend. If you decide to take the job you will be seeing a great deal more of him.'

'That would be nice,' said Renato, before continuing up the stairs.

Hearing Renato speak calmed Megan's initial fear. He seemed very normal, far less threatening than her prospective employer, and she wondered if she'd been making mountains out of molehills. If she really wanted to change her life, then she could do it by taking this job. The people here were unlike any people she'd ever met before. There was never any chance that she and Nick would have a discussion about Titian's paintings. It would be an opportunity for her to enter another

world, however briefly, and she knew that if she passed
it up she would regret it for the rest of her life, always
wondering what might have happened during the six
months of her employment.

Back in the library Fabrizio passed her a piece of
paper. 'I have written down the salary for this position.
Of course, your accommodation and food will be provided so you will have very little expenditure.'

Megan glanced at the piece of paper. 'It's very gen-
erous,' she said, trying to hide her astonishment.

'It's a very special position,' he said quietly. 'The
books are rare and the person I choose has to be trust-
worthy. Also, I need someone who will fit in with us all
here, someone who will wish to experience our way of
life to the full. Do you think you would like that,
Megan Stewart?'

Megan continued to look at the piece of paper on
which her salary was written. It was three times more
than she was earning now, which was utterly ridiculous, but again she sensed that it was part of the
honeyed trap. For some reason this man was anxious to
have Megan working for him, and even more anxious
for her to become a part of the household. Such an
opportunity was never going to come her way again

and she knew that any decision she took should be carefully considered, but she wasn't being offered the time needed. For once she would take a risk and live with the consequences. Lifting her head she looked directly at him.

'I'd like to read the contract through.'

'Of course.' Opening a drawer he pulled out several sheets of paper stapled together and handed them to her. Megan read it all, but absorbed none of it. She was too conscious of the fact that he was watching her, and out of the corner of her eye she could see one of his hands resting on the table top, his long, lean fingers tapping very lightly against the surface.

When she came to the end she nodded. 'It all looks fine. I've only one question.'

'Yes?'

'How many people live here with you?'

'As you already know, there is my sister Leonora and her lover Renato. My girlfriend also lives here, her name is Alessandra. Apart from that there is only my private secretary, Franco. Naturally we have some servants but you will not be mixing with them. You will make the numbers here even, three men and three women, something that is necessary at meal times. At the moment the ladies are outnumbered.' For the first time he smiled at her.

Megan was ashamed to realise that she was disappointed that he had a girlfriend living with him, although it was ridiculous to think that a man like him wouldn't have. Nevertheless, although a disappointment, it did take away some of her fears. He was hardly likely to have what her mother would have called 'wicked designs' on her if he was already living with someone. Whatever his reasons for wanting her so badly, they couldn't be too terrible. It was always possible that no one else had applied for the position.

'Well, are you going to take the plunge?' he asked quietly.

Megan hesitated for a split second and then nodded. 'If you're really offering me the post then yes, I would like to take it.'

'And you do understand that you have to stay for the full six months of the contract?'

'Yes. I take it you don't think I'll finish the work before then?'

'The task for which you are coming here will definitely take six months in order for it to be completed satisfactorily,' he replied.

It was only after she'd signed the contract and was driving home that Megan pondered Fabrizio's strangely worded answer to her question, but by then it was too late for her to back out. Not that she really wanted to, in fact she couldn't wait to start work the following week. All that remained now was for her to break the news to Nick.

Chapter Three

At eight o'clock that evening, as Megan and Nick were embroiled in a huge row over what she'd done, her future employer was sitting down to dinner. Fabrizio was interested to find out what his four companions thought of Megan.

His secretary, Franco, whose fair hair and blue eyes made him stand out from the other two men, dismissed her off-hand. 'She's typically English,' he remarked. 'So dowdy and with no dress sense. I can't imagine why a man like you, Fabrizio, a man who loves beautiful things around him, should choose her for this.'

Fabrizio shrugged. 'She's different, certainly, but I

regard her as a challenge. A considerable challenge,' he added with a sideways smile at Alessandra. Alessandra laughed in delight while Leonora looked questioningly at Renato.

'What did you think of her?' she asked her lover.

'From a personal point of view?'

Leonora nodded. 'Of course. Fabrizio will want us to join in his games as usual, will you not Fabrizio?' Her brother nodded. 'So, it's important to know what you thought.'

'I liked her,' he said firmly. 'Although her clothes were dowdy she had an attractive face, and she looked nice.'

'Nice!' Leonora gave a mocking laugh. 'Niceness isn't a quality that's needed here.'

'You asked me what I thought and I'm telling you,' said Renato calmly. 'I've no doubt we'll all get a lot of enjoyment from her. It will be a refreshing change, a new game.'

'You say this Megan will offer you a challenge,' continued Franco. 'What kind of a challenge could she possibly offer? She's a lost cause, the blood in her veins moves sluggishly, there's no passion in her.'

'Were you introduced to her?' asked Alessandra.

Franco shook his head. 'No, but I saw her, just as you did. We all saw her, Fabrizio made sure of that. Unfortunately, only Renato and Leonora were allowed to meet her.'

'I didn't want to meet her,' retorted Alessandra. 'This way it will be more fun when she comes here next week.'

'You ask what kind of a challenge she offers me,' said Fabrizio. 'I'll tell you. I wish to see if I can make her as decadent as the rest of us. To this end I have given her a tightly binding six-month contract. Within that six months I believe that I should succeed, but I will need the co-operation of everyone around this table tonight to help me achieve my goal. I trust I can rely on you all?'

Reactions around the table were varied. Leonora was obviously excited and she leant across to caress her lover's crotch. 'It will be fun, won't it, Renato?' she murmured, feeling him harden beneath the linen fabric of his trousers. 'I wonder if she has ever been dominated by a woman before?'

'She doesn't look as though she's been dominated by anyone,' said Renato, shifting slightly in his seat as Leonora scratched with her fingernails through the thin fabric and he felt himself growing even harder. 'Presumably she is not a virgin?'

Fabrizio shook his head. 'A virgin would be of no interest to me. She has a lover and believes that she knows about sexual matters. We will surprise her as we reveal her lack of true knowledge.'

'She doesn't look as though she's even heard of the things that excite you,' murmured Alessandra.

'Neither had you until we met,' Fabrizio reminded her. 'It is interesting though that now you are aware of them you cannot live without them.'

Alessandra flushed. 'Sometimes you take things too far,' she murmured.

Fabrizio shook his head. 'Nonsense. You like it all, Alessandra. Your body betrays you even when you protest. Besides, if you are unhappy, why are you still here with me?'

'I think it's going to be a wonderful six months,' announced Leonora.

'Now you'll have another person to dominate,' said Franco sharply. 'I'm not surprised you're looking forward to her coming. It must be boring being so much in control of Renato.'

'She isn't always in control of me,' retorted Renato.

'We're happy together,' said Leonora, shooting Franco a sharp look. 'You know nothing about our relationship.'

'I know a lot about *you,*' whispered Franco. Leonora glanced anxiously up the table. If her brother had overheard there would be trouble. Although he regarded Franco as an excellent secretary, he would be infuriated if he thought that such a trusted employee was harbouring a secret desire for his sister. Leonora knew of Franco's desire, but now was not the right moment to do anything about it. Besides, she and Renato were good together, and even better were the times they shared with Fabrizio and Alessandra.

'Then you'll all help me?' queried Fabrizio.

'Of course,' said Leonora.

'And you Alessandra?'

His lover nodded. 'It will be fun to see someone else travel along the same path that I've taken.'

'It won't be exactly the same path,' said Fabrizio. 'Megan Stewart is not as worldly wise as you were when we first met. Her descent into decadence will be far more shocking, and therefore all the more arousing for us. I trust that you will not attempt to undermine any of my efforts, Renato?' he added.

Renato shook his head. 'Why should I?'

'Because sometimes I know that you feel I go too far, but I do not wish to have the experiment spoilt by you. Do I have your word on this?'

Renato felt a fleeting moment of pity for the English girl, but he quickly suppressed it. 'You have my word. I too am looking forward to the next six months.'

'And you, Franco?'

The blond-haired man glanced at his employer. 'Will I be involved?'

Fabrizio looked thoughtful. 'I think that in this case, yes, you may be. After all, you are sometimes involved with Alessandra. Remember this morning?'

Alessandra's cheeks flushed. 'He hurt me this morning,' she complained.

'I saw what happened,' said Fabrizio smoothly.

'You left before it was over,' Alessandra protested.

'But I was there,' Leonora reminded her. 'You climaxed while he was punishing you. The pain turned you on, you can't deny it.'

Alessandra bit on her lower lip and for a second her eyes met Renato's across the table. He gave her a sympathetic glance but then looked quickly away, before Leonora could see.

'Is that true?' asked Fabrizio.

'Yes,' confessed Alessandra.

'Then why are you complaining? Remember, we must be very careful how we begin. Initially, Megan Stewart must believe that her only sexual experiences here will be with me. Once she is thoroughly mine, then she will begin to learn the truth about us all, and hopefully about herself.'

'What if you're wrong about her?' asked Leonora. 'What if she simply isn't turned on by pain and humiliation?'

'I am not wrong,' said Fabrizio firmly. 'Have I ever been wrong before? Was I wrong about you, Alessandra?' He stroked his lover's cheek with the backs of his fingers and she nibbled at each of his fingertips in turn, her breathing growing more rapid as he slid his ring finger inside her mouth, allowing her to suck on it before withdrawing it and kissing her lightly on her bare shoulder. 'No, I was not wrong about you and I am not wrong about our English librarian either.'

The conversation then turned to other things, but when dinner was finally over they did not go into the drawing room for coffee, as was usual. Instead, Fabrizio led Alessandra away upstairs to their room and a few seconds later Leonora and Renato also vanished, leaving Franco alone at the table.

Surprisingly his thoughts were not of the young English girl who was to join them but of the blonde-haired Leonora, who he desired so much that he could think of nothing else day or night. It was a dangerous obsession and he knew it, but he was helplessly enthralled by her and determined that eventually he would possess her.

Closing the bedroom door behind him, Renato turned to face Leonora. He wanted to undress her, to lay her on the bed and cover her whole body with his tongue and his mouth, watching her pleasure peak time after time, but as usual Leonora had other ideas. She held up a warning hand.

'Don't touch me. Stand where you are, I'm going to undress you.'

Although there were times when she allowed him to take command, Leonora generally preferred to be in control, and Renato was amazed at how exciting the sex always was when she did this. He stood motionless as she removed his jacket and then her fingers were tearing at his shirt, almost ripping the buttons off in her haste, but when he instinctively lifted a hand to help her she stepped back from him. 'If you do that again I'm going to stop,' she cautioned him.

By the time he was naked he was already fully aroused and Leonora knelt down in front of him. She took him into her mouth and sucked gently on the tip of his erection before leading him to the bed and pushing him face down across it. He gave a muffled groan as he felt her fingers parting his buttocks and then she slowly inserted a finger deep inside him, until she was able to massage the tiny gland so that he instantly became even harder. He was aching with need now and wriggled against the soft duvet. His reward for that was a stinging slap with her hand across his buttocks, and when he yelped she laughed with delight.

'Turn over,' she commanded him, and as he obeyed her eyes swept down the length of him. 'You really want me, don't you?' she said with pleasure.

'You know I do.' His voice was thick with desire.

'You're so large. I always forget how big you are,' she marvelled.

'Don't you want me inside you?' he begged.

'Not yet. The fun's only just beginning.' With that she fetched a thin strip of leather which she then tied around the base of his erection, and he realised with horror that she intended to keep him hard for as long as possible. 'There,' she said with satisfaction. 'Now I can use you and there's nothing you can do about it until I release you.'

Renato didn't like this game; it made his testicles ache and often Leonora would keep him waiting nearly an hour before he was allowed his pleasure, although when that pleasure came it was incredibly intense.

She made him move around until he was lying with his head on the pillows and then she pulled up her skirt, revealing that she wasn't wearing any panties and straddled his hips, bending her head forward so that her long blonde hair teased his nipples. Gradually she moved down his body, turning her head from side to side so that every centimetre of his flesh was caressed by her hair's silken touch. Eventually she turned around so that her back was to him, and bending forward she began to lick at the tiny drop of clear fluid at the tip of his erection. Having teased it off she continued licking until he thought he was going to explode.

'I think I'd like you inside me now,' she announced abruptly, and climbing slowly on top she impaled herself on him, allowing him only slightly inside her and using her powerful legs to help her rise and fall until he heard her whimper with delight and saw her body shudder.

Despite his best intentions, Renato began to move his hips as well and he heard himself moan softly as the incredible tightness in his testicles increased, while a dull ache spread upwards through his belly.

'You're not meant to move,' said Leonora sharply, lifting herself off him and leaving him without any stimulation. 'Just for that you'll have to wait a little longer.'

He stared up at her, trying not to let her see how desperately he needed her.

Leonora licked her lips. 'I love looking at you when you're like this,' she said throatily. 'Your body's so beautiful, especially when it's covered with sweat. Tell me the truth, have you ever felt like this about another woman?'

'Never,' said Renato with total honesty.

'Tell me how much you need me,' she ordered.

'I'd have thought you could see that for yourself.'

Frowning, Leonora walked away from the bed and returned with a riding crop in her hand. 'That wasn't what I meant,' she said sharply, and lifting her hand she flicked the crop. He felt the sting of it across his tender belly. For a moment there was a blaze of red hot pain, a heat that almost immediately turned into incredible pleasure which mingled with the throbbing ache of his frustration, so that it felt as though every nerve in his body was stretched to breaking point. 'Now tell me properly,' said Leonora.

'I need your gorgeous body,' he cried. 'I want to plunge myself inside you, to fuck you until you scream for mercy. I want to make you come and come until you can't come any more. For God's sake take this leather strap off me and let me do what I want.'

Leonora smiled a tiny, cat-like smile. 'That's better. But are you just saying it because you know it's what I like to hear, or because you mean it?'

'Because I mean it,' he gasped, wondering how much longer he could stand this kind of torture.

'I'm not sure I believe you.' Slowly, Leonora stripped off all her clothes and then once more straddled his thighs, wriggling on the tops of his legs so that he could feel her soaking vulva against his bare flesh. She rocked backwards and forwards, stimulating her clitoris and uttering tiny sighs of contentment before bending herself forward and once more taking him into her mouth.

She swirled her tongue around his shaft and sucked lightly until the pain was unbearable.

'For God's sake, Leonora, untie me. You've no idea how much this hurts.'

'Oh, yes I have,' said Leonora happily. 'That's why I'm enjoying myself so much. Poor Renato, let me lick your testicles for you, that might help the ache.'

'No, it won't,' he protested, but she ignored him. She began to lick and suck on the swollen testicles, taking each one into her mouth in turn and nibbling with exquisite delicacy on the agonisingly sensitive flesh. Renato lay completely still, hardly daring to breath. She'd never gone this far before. The restriction around the base of his erection was normally removed much sooner than this, and the ache of thwarted need was beginning to spread down his groin. All he wanted to do was push into her, release himself inside her in a spasm of ecstasy. The more she licked and sucked the worse the ache grew, and the more his excitement grew too. Eventually, just as he decided that he couldn't take any more, she lifted her head and he felt her hands fumbling at the leather strap.

'There,' she said huskily. 'Now you can do all those things you wanted to do.'

Released from his servitude Renato grabbed hold of his lover and, pushing her onto her back with surprising force, he pulled her legs savagely apart and rammed himself straight inside her.

Leonora was soaking wet, fully aroused by all that she'd done to him, and this only increased his desire to turn the tables and briefly dominate her. He rolled over so that he was on his side and pulled her body hard against his. She gave a tiny cry of surprise as he pushed two fingers between the cheeks of her bottom and pressed them hard against the inner walls of her rectum while at the same time continuing to thrust in and out of her. His left arm was beneath her, circling her waist and keeping her tightly against him. Because she was so small he was able to force her into the rhythm he wanted as they rolled around the bed.

Leonora abruptly climaxed, taking him by surprise, and as he felt the tight, hot walls of her vagina contract around him he knew that he was soon going to come. Immediately he withdrew his fingers from her rectum and pushed her onto her back, pinioning her arms above her head with one hand and savagely gripping her left breast with the other as he drove relentlessly in and out of her. She was screaming with fury now, fury that he'd turned the tables and that she was not controlling the way things were going, but Renato was past caring. All the waiting that she'd forced him to endure, all the desperate aching need for release drove him on.

After he'd finally spilt himself inside Leonora he collapsed on top of her, keeping his hips moving so that his pubic bone put pressure on her clitoris, causing her to spasm once more and milk the very last drops from him. Reluctantly he released her, suddenly replete, and he turned onto his side with his back towards her.

'What's the matter?' asked Leonora. 'You looked as though you enjoyed that.'

'I did.'

'Then kiss me,' she demanded.

'I don't want to kiss you.'

'I've made you cross, haven't I?' She sounded pleased rather than worried.

'You kept me waiting too long,' he muttered.

Leonora ran a finger down his spine and he shivered. 'But you loved it. I've never seen you so hard and you've never taken me like that before. It really turned you on, so why are you complaining?'

Renato didn't know why he didn't want to kiss her. She was right; it had been a fantastic experience, but being the kind of person she was she couldn't understand why he sometimes wanted things to be a little different. On the other hand, the last thing he wanted was to lose her and he quickly turned to face her again. 'I'm just tired,' he lied.

'Let's see how tired you really are,' she murmured as she began kissing him deeply and passionately. It wasn't very long before she slid a hand down his body and to his amazement he realised that he was already stirring again. 'There, I knew you weren't that tired,' she whispered, her fingers stroking the creases at the tops of his thighs. 'We're good together, you know that. I can't wait for the English girl to join us.'

Much later, after they'd made love again and Leonora was asleep, Renato thought about what she had said. He wondered how the naïve, unworldly-looking girl that he'd seen on the stairs was going to cope in this house. It wouldn't be easy, but Fabrizio was a good judge of character and Renato had to believe that he was right about her, and that in time she, like Alessandra before her, would learn to enjoy the kind of domination games that the Balocchi family were so fond of.

*

The master bedroom was filled with Alessandra's loud moans. She was sitting on the edge of a tall Queen Anne chair, her arms handcuffed behind her back and the blindfold once more over her eyes. Fabrizio was kneeling on the floor in front of her, his hands gripping the cheeks of her bottom, lifting her upwards so that he could lick and suck at the soaking flesh of her vulva. Sometimes his tongue would dart inside her, at other times swirl around her tight, throbbing clitoris. Occasionally he would pause and press his mouth over the entire area in the most intimate kiss that he could give her. She'd never been so wet and was writhing frantically.

'Hurry up and let me come,' she pleaded with him. 'I shall go mad in a minute.' But Fabrizio only laughed deep in his throat and continued his skilful arousal. Time and again he brought her to the brink of release only to remove his mouth for a few seconds, leaving her hips jerking frantically upwards as she fought for that final touch that would topple her into a climax.

As he removed his mouth yet again she cried out with impatience, and then suddenly uttered a tiny scream as she felt something being pushed inside her, not Fabrizio's swollen penis but something much larger and smoother, something so large that it stretched her more than she'd ever been stretched before. She realised that it must be one of the marble dildos that he collected, but this was the first time he'd used one of this size on her. Although she was aching to be filled, this was so large that the sensation crossed the threshold from pleasure to pain and she began to whimper in protest.

Immediately, the thick, smooth dildo stopped moving and was withdrawn a fraction, but now she felt bereft and her body's delicious climb towards orgasm was halted. 'No, don't stop,' she begged.

'You didn't seem to like it.'

'It felt too big.'

'It's what you need, but you're ashamed to admit it. I'd have thought that by now you were past being ashamed of anything.'

She wanted to argue with him, to explain that it wasn't shame that was making her protest, it was his constant need to make her accept only pleasure that was tinged with pain that was frustrating her. She didn't say anything though because her body was screaming for release, and she could feel the sticky dampness between her thighs betraying her. Fabrizio licked some of her juices away, while at the same time ramming the thick marble column deeply inside her again, and her back arched away from the chair as her body finally spasmed in an ecstasy of pleasure.

Almost as savagely as it had been pushed into her the marble column was wrenched out of her, her handcuffs removed, and Fabrizio was lifting her up and carrying her across the room. She wished that he'd remove the blindfold because when she couldn't see him, no matter what he was doing, there was always a frisson of fear in her pleasure; fear that sharpened the sensations, fear of the unknown.

As her back was pressed against the bedroom wall she wrapped her long legs around his waist and at last he began to thrust himself inside her, his hips moving in a tantalisingly slow and steady rhythm. Despite her sobs and pleas he refused to hurry, and she knew that once more he was taking pleasure from delaying her satisfaction. Hesitantly she wrapped her arms around him and felt his lips against the side of her neck, touching the pulse that was beating wildly there.

'Imagine what the English girl will be like by the time we have her doing this,' he murmured. 'How will she react do you think? Will her body tremble as yours does? Will her juices flow as much, or does she lack your passion?'

All the time he was talking he was increasing the rhythm of his thrusts and electric thrills ran upwards through Alessandra's belly and breasts. She heard Fabrizio's breathing quicken and felt him begin to shake. Knowing that his climax was near she grew frantic that she'd miss her own and thrust her hips outwards from the wall, grinding herself against him. They came together, both uttering cries of pleasure, but Alessandra's cries carried on long after Fabrizio's because, as the last ripples of her orgasm died away, he abruptly closed his mouth around her aching left breast and bit the tip of the tiny, tender nipple.

Her scream was as much of pleasure as of pain because this was something that she'd learnt to adore. Even as the sound of her cry was still echoing round the room, her body rippled with a final orgasm that left her utterly exhausted.

Only now did Fabrizio remove the blindfold and put her down on the floor. Gazing about her she tried to adjust her eyes to the light and saw that Fabrizio was lying on the bed, watching her carefully. 'So tell me, can

you imagine our English librarian in your place?' he
asked.

Alessandra couldn't. From this very bedroom window
she'd seen the young English girl getting out of her car.
There had been nothing about her to suggest any kind
of sensuality or latent eroticism. She couldn't think for
one moment that the girl would enjoy the dark pleasure-
pain that Fabrizio was so good at inflicting, or that she
would be able to give the total submission to his will
that he so frequently demanded. 'No,' she said slowly.
'I don't think you will be able to make her decadent.'

'And you're not jealous?'

Alessandra's large violet eyes, which were part of the
reason for her success as a model on the catwalks of
Milan, widened in surprise. She'd tried very hard to
hide her disquiet at the thought of another woman tem-
porarily taking her place, but it seemed that she hadn't
fully succeeded. 'A little,' she confessed, knowing that
Fabrizio would despise her if she lied.

'But won't you enjoy corrupting her? Inflicting on
her some of the punishments that have been inflicted on
you in order to make you a perfect companion for me?'

Alessandra nodded. 'Yes, that will be pleasing, but if
I'm so perfect why do you need her?'

Fabrizio sighed. 'I get bored too easily. I need constant diversions, new games to play all the time. That's what Megan Stewart is; a game, a small diversion, nothing more.'

'In that case I must make sure that her tuition is as strict as mine was,' said Alessandra.

Fabrizio nodded. 'That will please me greatly. If anything, I wish her training to be even stricter. However, you must understand that we cannot begin the game properly until I have her in the palm of my hand.'

'Meaning what?'

'Meaning that I alone will seduce her the first time.' Alessandra began to frown. 'Don't worry,' laughed Fabrizio. 'You will all be watching, only the English girl won't know it. Now come to bed, it's time for us to sleep. We will go away for the next couple of days, fly to Tuscany and enjoy ourselves as other lovers do. When we return next week the fun will really begin.'

Alessandra smiled to herself. The fun might begin for them, but for Megan it was going to be a very different story.

Chapter Four

Megan arrived at the Sussex house late on the Monday afternoon. She was surprised at how much luggage she'd brought, but since her interview she'd been on a special shopping expedition for more interesting clothes, anxious to erase what she knew must be her original impression of dowdiness.

As a footman carried her bags inside and up to her bedroom she was welcomed by a beautiful, tall girl whose tawny hair framed an olive-skinned face that was dominated by a pair of large violet eyes. Her face seemed vaguely familiar to Megan, although she couldn't imagine how she could have met anyone so beautiful without remembering where.

The girl held out her hand. 'Welcome. I'm Alessandra, Fabrizio's girlfriend. He's out at the moment seeing his solicitors but will be home by dinner time. He asked me to offer his apologies and welcome you in his place. I trust you had a good journey here?'

'The traffic wasn't too bad, although I'd hoped to arrive half an hour earlier.'

Alessandra smiled. 'It doesn't matter. No one expects you to start work until tomorrow. Do you really enjoy working with books?' she added curiously.

Megan nodded. 'I've loved reading ever since I was a little girl. By the time I was ten I knew I wanted to be a librarian. I realise that sounds very boring but that's the kind of child I was. Perhaps it's because I was an only one, and my parents were quite elderly. My mother was forty when she had me.'

'An only child,' mused Alessandra. 'I'm one of eight so I find that difficult to comprehend.'

'It probably sounds ridiculous but I can't help feeling that I've met you before,' said Megan.

Alessandra shook her head. 'I don't think we've met, but you may have seen me in magazines. I do quite a lot of modelling for the top fashion designers on the Continent.'

'Of course!' exclaimed Megan. 'I've seen you in the magazines at the hairdressers.'

'You've got beautiful hair,' said Alessandra, reaching out and touching the long brown curls. 'Does it wave naturally?'

'Yes. It's quite difficult to do anything with it except wear it like this. I'd love to have hair like yours,' she added, looking at the other girl's long, sleek hair that fell to below her shoulders.

'But why? Your hair is beautiful. And you should wear more make-up. If you emphasised your eyes you could be beautiful too.'

Megan felt very embarrassed. 'I don't think even my mother would ever have considered me a potential beauty, although it's kind of you to say so. I've never seen the point of wearing much make-up. When I do, I look like a painted doll.'

'Then while you are staying with us I will show you how,' said Alessandra. 'We will aim for the natural look, but of course it will not be natural which is the whole point of the exercise. I'm really looking forward to your stay,' she continued, leading Megan into the house. 'I have a feeling we're going to become very good friends.'

Megan was slightly taken aback by the other girl's enthusiasm. 'I imagine I'm going to be busy working most of the time.'

Alessandra shook her head. 'Nonsense. In the day perhaps, but Fabrizio will not expect you to work in the evenings or at weekends.'

'I think he does expect me to work at weekends. He certainly made it clear that he didn't want me returning to Lincolnshire more often than was strictly necessary.'

Alessandra gave her a curious look, half amused and half pitying. 'That was not because he wished you to work in the library, but because he wished you to integrate completely into our unit here.'

'I see,' said Megan, who didn't see at all. Alessandra continued chattering in a friendly fashion all the way up to the bedroom, then showed Megan everything that she thought she needed to see before leaving her to unpack in peace.

'Dinner is at eight, but we always meet up in the small drawing room for a drink about fifteen minutes beforehand,' she explained.

'What should I wear?' asked Megan, uncertain as to how formal the dinners were.

'Why, anything you like. We girls always try to look beautiful for the men, but evening dresses are not required.' She gave a gurgle of laughter.

Megan didn't feel that the reply had helped her very much. She knew that she was going to feel horribly out of place at the meal. She could still remember how attractive Fabrizio's sister was, and the thought of sitting at a table with her and the stunning Alessandra was daunting.

After she'd unpacked she took a bath in the deep tub, using the bath oil and one of the body lotions that stood on the glass shelves in beautifully coloured glass bottles. When it was nearly time to go down for dinner she decided that there was no point in trying to compete with the other two women and put on a simple, ankle-length V-neck dress in a lilac floral print with a small slit at the back. Surveying herself in the full-length mirror that stood at the far end of the room she decided that it suited her, although it rather emphasised her full breasts, something that she normally avoided doing whenever possible as they seemed out of proportion to the rest of her body.

Once she was downstairs in the hallway she hesitated, uncertain as to where she should go. A maid quickly materialised out of thin air and with a smile opened one of the numerous doors leading off the corridor and gestured for Megan to enter. The room was about half the size of the drawing room Fabrizio had shown Megan during her interview, but was furnished in a similar style, although this time the colour scheme was far darker, the furnishings and curtains all a deep burgundy with tiny cream flowers.

There were already five people in the room and Megan realised that her entrance completed the group. Fabrizio, who had been standing at the far end talking animatedly to a blond-haired man, came towards her with a welcoming smile. 'Alessandra told me you arrived safely. I think that the only person here whom you have not met is my secretary, Franco, is it not?'

Megan nodded. Fabrizio lifted a hand and gestured for Franco to join them. Megan was surprised by his fair hair. On the other hand he was tanned, as she expected Italian men to be, whereas Fabrizio was very pale. She assumed that this was because he came from northern Italy, where the physical characteristics were slightly different.

Franco was not as tall as either his employer or Leonora's boyfriend but he was more heavily built, with broad shoulders, the muscles at the tops of his arms showing through the jacket of his suit. Although he smiled, his blue eyes remained cold. Taking Megan's hand he bent over it and kissed the tips of her fingers. 'Welcome,' he said quietly. 'We've all been looking forward to your arrival.'

Megan couldn't imagine why. Getting the library straight hardly seemed to warrant such extravagant compliments. On the other hand she supposed this could be their way of making her feel welcome, and it was working because she didn't feel nearly as uncomfortable as she'd expected. This was despite the fact that Alessandra looked incredibly elegant in a sleeveless, two-tiered A-line dress, the burnt tangerine colour a perfect foil for her olive skin and tawny hair, whilst Leonora was wearing a black dress that was so tight it looked like a second skin. Although full-length it was slashed from ankle to thigh on the left-hand side and she was wearing incredibly high heels, emphasising her perfect calf muscles.

'What can I get you to drink?' asked Franco.

Megan hesitated. She wasn't a great one for drinking and when out with Nick and his friends often drank lager. However, she knew instinctively that there would be no lager in this house, even for the men. 'Perhaps a sherry,' she muttered.

'Dry or sweet?'

Again she hesitated.

'Why not try one of the dry Spanish sherries,' suggested Fabrizio. 'They are a delicious aperitif, particularly when drunk with ice. If you are not accustomed to drinking sherry it might be a good idea to have it with ice.'

'That sounds very nice,' said Megan, who didn't have a clue whether it would be nice or not. This was one area in which she had no knowledge at all and she hoped that she wasn't going to be asked to choose her own wine at dinner. When she took her first mouthful of the sherry she coughed and tears sprang to her eyes. It was so dry that it burnt the back of her throat.

'You must sip it, not gulp it,' laughed Alessandra. 'It is an acquired taste, but you should persevere. Most of our white wines are dry. I hope you will enjoy those more.'

Megan hoped so, too, as she took a second, more cautious sip from her glass. By the time they went through to dinner she was beginning to enjoy the taste.

'You learn very quickly,' whispered Fabrizio, ushering her through to the dining room. 'At least you are willing to try new experiences.'

Throughout dinner the conversation centred mainly on Leonora's horses, of which Megan gathered she had three, and their chances in a forthcoming riding competition. Apart from that, Renato asked Megan about her work in the library and Leonora asked about Nick.

'Does your boyfriend mind you coming to stay with us for six months?' she asked over coffee.

'He wasn't very pleased,' confessed Megan, who felt that it might be unwise to tell this group of complete strangers that Nick had been so angry he'd broken off their relationship, and so she had no one who would worry about her if she didn't call.

'Perhaps he's afraid that you will not care for him so much when you return to Lincolnshire,' said Leonora. 'You're bound to be changed by your stay here.'

'I doubt that,' replied Megan. 'I am used to working with books. In what way do you think that I'll change?'

'You will change simply by being with us,' said Fabrizio smoothly. 'Tonight you have sampled a new drink and tasted different food. Later on there will be more things for you to discover, more fresh sensations for you to experience. You cannot possibly return to this Nick the same person that you were when you left him. It would be a great waste of your stay if you did. In fact, we are all going to make quite sure that such a thing does not happen. Is that not true everyone?' He glanced around the table.

The other men and women looked at Megan intently and she felt very strange. It was as though they were devouring her with their eyes, as though in some strange way she was fulfilling a need in them simply by being there. She couldn't imagine what that need could be. 'Then I must try not to disappoint you,' she said lightly, trying to break the atmosphere that had descended.

'Indeed,' agreed Fabrizio. 'Now, you look a little tired. No doubt you would like to retire early after your drive here.' He rose to his feet and opened the door. It was clearly a dismissal, although a very polite one, and Megan assumed he wished to talk to the others about personal matters.

'I am tired,' she agreed. 'Thank you very much for the warm welcome you've all given me, and for the delicious meal. I look forward to having another sherry tomorrow night,' she added, glancing up at Fabrizio from beneath lowered lashes. She was astonished by the expression that she caught on his face before he realised that she was looking at him. There was satisfaction there but also, and she was certain that she wasn't mistaken, there was desire, a desire that made her stomach turn over with incredulous excitement. Hastily she left and hurried to her room.

'You're being utterly ridiculous,' she chided herself as she undressed and slid between the sheets. 'He was probably thinking about Alessandra, not you.'

All the same there'd been something strange about the dinner, about all of them and their attitudes towards her. If she hadn't been so tired, and so relaxed by the unaccustomed drink, she might have been worried.

Fabrizio's dark, heavy-lidded eyes glittered with excitement as he looked around the table. 'What do you think of her now?' he asked the other four.

'I can't wait to begin,' said Leonora excitedly. 'She's incredible, so unaroused and yet you can tell she's eager to please. Won't it be wonderful, Renato?'

Renato looked doubtful. 'I'm not certain that she was the right choice,' he said at last.

'How fortunate that I brought you to England because of your business brain,' said Fabrizio sharply. 'You're not a very good judge of women.'

'On the contrary, I'm an excellent judge of women, as Leonora will testify,' said Renato smoothly. 'It is merely that I feel you've made a mistake this time. Alessandra, do you agree with me?'

Alessandra hesitated. 'I've never known Fabrizio to be wrong,' she said eventually.

'But you're not convinced, are you?' persisted Renato.

'She's not at all like me,' admitted Alessandra. 'Although I was a novice in many ways, I had also had many lovers and done far more than this girl can ever have done. What will she have learnt about sensuality and eroticism shut away in her dull little library in the fenlands?'

'That's precisely why I chose her.' Fabrizio sounded impatient. 'Perhaps I found you too easy to tutor, Alessandra. Maybe that is why I have become bored.'

Alessandra was clearly hurt by his remark. 'But if you've misjudged her she will leave. Then there will be no game, and no fun for any of us.'

'Are you saying that Renato's right?'

Alessandra shook her head. 'No, I'm not certain that he's right but I sense he may be. She isn't like me. I was in love with you before our affair began. There is nothing to hold her here if she takes fright.'

'She won't take fright, as long as we go carefully,' said Fabrizio. 'I'm surprised and disappointed in you two,' he added, glancing first at Alessandra and then at Renato. 'You appear faint-hearted about this whole enterprise. Maybe I can understand it with you, *cara*,' he added, looking at his lover. 'Naturally you are nervous that she will take up too much of my time, but you, Renato, what is your excuse?'

'I don't need an excuse,' said Renato. 'I tell you what though, as you're so certain you're right, let's have a bet on it.'

'A wager?'

'That's right.'

'What are the terms of this wager?'

'I don't believe that you will succeed in changing her so that she becomes one of us, not even within six months. I believe that either she'll leave before her contract is up, or that when she goes you will have failed.'

'How much are you willing to bet on it?' asked Fabrizio.

'A thousand pounds?'

'Not very sure of yourself then.'

Renato sighed. 'Five thousand?'

Fabrizio nodded. 'Yes, that makes it more fun. You're sure you can afford to lose that much?'

Renato flushed. 'I take that as an insult.'

Fabrizio nodded. 'I apologise. I was not for one moment doubting your ability to pay, although it should concern me because you will most certainly have to.'

Renato shook his head. 'You can't be that certain, no one can.'

'I'm certain we'll succeed,' said Leonora. 'Fabrizio believes that English women are exciting because under their innocent façade lie hidden depths of passion. I think he's right, and I also think that Megan will surprise you, Renato.'

'There is one thing,' said Fabrizio. 'Although I'm happy for the wager to take place I still expect you to do your utmost to make sure my little game works, Renato.'

'Of course. Surely you know me well enough to know that I would not behave dishonourably.'

Leonora laughed. 'How seriously you two are taking this game. For me it is merely a diversion, some fun.'

'That's because you're like your brother, easily bored,' said Franco, making his voice heard for the first time.

'I'm not bored at the moment,' said Leonora, glancing briefly at him.

'No? Then why are you looking forward to this so much? Renato alone is obviously no longer enough to keep you entertained.'

Renato half rose to his feet but Fabrizio gestured for him to sit down. 'Tell me Franco, what do you think of our new resident?'

'I think her initiation will be most enjoyable,' said Franco coolly. 'There will be times when she'll be very afraid and ...'

'And you can't wait to see that, can you?' Renato concluded for him.

Leonora watched the two men closely, paying particular attention to Franco. She was well aware that he lusted after her, and she was equally aware that her brother would never stand for such a liaison. Unfortunately this only made it an even more attractive proposition for her, although for the moment Renato and the prospect of the games they were all going to play with Megan were more than enough to keep her happy. Still, there was something about Franco that fascinated her. She sensed that he would be difficult to dominate, and she loved a challenge.

'Tomorrow I shall begin my initial seduction,' said Fabrizio. 'It will no doubt take several days, but when I finally take her it will be upstairs in the playroom so that you can all watch through the two-way mirror.'

Alessandra smiled. 'I look forward to that,' she murmured.

'And I'm looking forward to this evening,' said Fabrizio, getting to his feet and catching hold of Alessandra's hand. 'Come Leonora, Renato, let us retire upstairs to the top floor. There we will enjoy ourselves to the full and with good fortune some of the sounds will carry to Megan's bedroom. She will not fully understand them, but they should arouse in her a mixture of confusion and excitement which will serve me well tomorrow. From now on all her senses should be stimulated as much as possible. She is hungry to learn about art, food and wine. From there it is but a short step to a very different kind of hunger.'

After he'd finished speaking he and Alessandra left the room, together with Leonora and Renato, and once again Franco was alone. He sat in silence, sipping his brandy and thinking about Leonora. When she'd glanced at him tonight there had definitely been a spark of interest in her eyes, something more than she'd ever shown him before, and he wondered if he could somehow use the new situation in the house to his own advantage.

It was clear that Renato wasn't entirely happy about what was going to happen to the English girl. If, as a result, he displayed any kind of weakness then Leonora would begin to despise him, giving Franco an opportunity to move in. As for Fabrizio's opposition, that was something Franco would deal with when the time came. He knew a lot about the Balocchis, not just in his capacity as secretary to Fabrizio but also because they had, from time to time, allowed him to join in their games of debauchery. If he had to he would use that knowledge to prevent Fabrizio from keeping him away from his sister.

Even thinking about the voluptuous blonde girl had made Franco hard, and when he went up to bed later he took one of the maids with him. She was attractive enough in her own way and always compliant to his will, although even she was taken aback by the savage way he made love to her and the number of times he took her during the night. He knew that she was flattered, and this amused him because if she'd realised that all the time he was imagining Leonora crying out beneath him and pleading for respite, then she wouldn't have felt flattered at all.

When Megan came down to breakfast the next morning she didn't feel quite as fresh as she'd hoped. Although she'd got off to sleep quickly she'd been woken several times during the night by strange keening sounds from another room. She'd never heard sounds quite like them, and in her sleep-filled brain the cries had occasionally become mixed with what sounded like gasps of ecstasy and muffled protests. Drifting in and out of sleep, her mind curiously aroused by the noises and her dreams unusually sensual, Megan had felt disorientated. Now, in the broad light of day, she wondered if the noises had been real or not. She didn't quite see how they could have been when no one appeared to be using the upper floor except for herself.

Only Fabrizio was still at the table, the cluttered plates at the other place settings bearing testimony to the fact that the rest of the household had already eaten and gone. 'I trust you slept well?' he asked with a smile as he got to his feet.

'Very well thank you,' she lied.

'Are you sure? You look a little tired.'

'I'm afraid I'm not a morning person.'

'That must have been a disadvantage in a public library,' he said dryly.

'I was quite lucky in that respect. The library didn't open until ten, although we were meant to get in earlier and tidy up. I'm afraid I was quite often a little late,' she added apologetically.

Fabrizio made a tutting sound of mock disapproval. 'You didn't mention that during our interview.'

'You didn't ask me,' Megan pointed out.

'As soon as you've eaten I'll take you along to the library and you can get started,' he said as she nibbled on some toast, wondering why it was that even the sight of him was enough to tighten her stomach and make eating difficult.

Half an hour later she stood staring at the chaos of the room as the Italian showed her a catalogue of the books that were all somewhere within the library.

'I'm afraid I've no idea which ones are on the shelves and which ones on the floor,' he confessed. 'My uncle was in the process of re-organising when he died. He was one of those people who hated to delegate, which is fine in theory but not if you fail to do the things yourself. What's the point of money if you're not willing to pay anyone to do the tedious things for you? I believe that life is to be lived to the full if possible.'

'I suppose so,' agreed Megan, who'd never been able to afford even a cleaning woman for her tiny flat.

Fabrizio smiled at her and for a brief moment his hand touched her shoulder. Her skin seemed to burn beneath the crisp white cotton blouse that she was wearing.

'Well, the sooner I get started the better.'

'There's no hurry. You do have six months. I'll come back later and see how you're getting on. If you want a coffee, or need anything at all, pull on the bell-rope over there. One of the maids will answer it.'

Once the door was closed behind him Megan sank down onto the nearest chair. 'What's the matter with you?' she asked herself fiercely. 'You're not some silly twelve-year-old, going weak at the knees over a film star, you're a twenty-three-year-old woman and it's time you pulled yourself together.'

Despite her words, Megan couldn't help the way she

felt. Never before had she reacted to a man's touch the way she'd reacted to Fabrizio's. As for his smiles, rare as they were, they filled her with an insane desire to have him take her in his arms and smile at her with love and desire rather than politeness. The fact that he had a girlfriend as beautiful as Alessandra made these dreams completely ridiculous, yet at times Megan could have sworn that he was interested in her, that she wasn't simply imagining it in order to sustain a fantasy. In the end she forced herself to put all thoughts of her new employer to the back of her mind and get on with her work.

All of the books were in excellent condition, Some of them, whilst interesting, were worthless; others though were first editions and Megan knew that a few were extremely valuable. She decided that the sooner she could get a list to an antique book dealer the better. She must make sure that the more valuable books were on the highest shelves, if possible, safely out of harm's reach.

She'd been working for nearly half an hour when she heard the sound of a horse's hooves. Walking over to the tall, narrow window that looked out on the grounds at the back of the house she saw Leonora dismounting from an extremely large and strong-looking chestnut gelding. The animal was magnificent, and so too was its rider. Again Megan admired Leonora in her riding outfit. She was holding on to the horse's bridle and looking back over her shoulder, laughing at someone. Megan was about to move away from the window when Renato appeared, and for a moment the young couple stood together by the horse's head talking animatedly, their hands moving rapidly in the air in what Megan was beginning to realise was a typically Italian fashion.

All at once Leonora caught hold of Renato's arm and pulled him towards her, while at the same time her free hand began to unfasten the buttons of her riding jacket. Transfixed, Megan stood silently by the window and watched as, with a brisk slap on its rump, Leonora sent the horse on its way to the stable so that she and Renato were alone.

The blonde girl continued to pull her lover with her until her back was resting against a large oak tree. By this time her jacket had been thrown to the ground and Renato was undoing her riding shirt. To Megan's astonishment Leonora wore no bra and her beautifully rounded breasts sprang free as he pushed the material to one side and began to suck greedily on her nipples.

Megan's stomach lurched. She felt the palms of her hands begin to sweat. She knew that she should move away, that she had no right to be watching, but there was something about the urgency of Leonora's passion that was riveting. Renato continued to kiss and caress his lover's breasts while Leonora moved her hips seductively against the tree, reaching forward to unfasten Renato's trousers. Within seconds his erection had sprung free and he lunged forward, clearly eager to penetrate his lover.

To Megan's surprise Leonora twisted away from him, and now he was the one with his back against the tree. Laughing, Leonora shrugged off her shirt so that her upper torso was completely naked. She rubbed herself teasingly against Renato's chest, bare now because she'd opened his shirt, and Megan could see his rigid erection harden even more. His hands moved to grab Leonora but, to Megan's astonishment, she slapped them away. Amazingly, Renato accepted what she'd done. Now he stood passively against the tree, his hands at his sides, as Leonora slid to her knees and drew his massive erection into her mouth.

As Leonora's lips and tongue began to work on him, Megan realised that she was shamefully damp between her thighs. The white cotton fabric of her panties was sticking to her and as Leonora's head moved back and forth Megan lifted her skirt, and almost without realising it began to move her fingers between her thighs, tickling her rapidly hardening clitoris through the material.

Renato's hips were moving constantly back and forth as he thrust in and out of Leonora's mouth, trying desperately to set the rhythm himself, but every time he did this Leonora moved her mouth away and, consumed with frustration, he would have to stand still again before she'd resume her arousal of him.

Megan found the frustration almost as unbearable as Renato evidently did. Her own excitement was rising, delicious hot tingles sparking through her lower belly. She was caught up in the sensations of the couple she was watching; and watching secretly which only made it all the more arousing. At one point, when Leonora moved away from her lover, Megan saw Renato gesticulate angrily and for a moment she was forced to stop pleasuring herself as the couple appeared to be on the point of separating.

Then, luckily for Megan, the argument was resolved and Leonora finally allowed Renato to push her against the tree once more.

However, when he was at last able to thrust inside her – the violence of the movement causing her to rise up on her toes – Leonora lifted her hands and, bending her fingers so that they looked like cats' claws, scratched furiously at his naked chest and upper abdomen. Megan saw Renato flinch as his lover's nails first made contact with his flesh, but surprisingly her own flesh quickened in response and she felt her pleasure rising to a delicious crescendo.

The couple in the garden were now locked together in a ferocious coupling of a kind that Megan had never imagined possible. Renato was driving into Leonora with all his strength and she was responding by tearing at him, her head thrown back and her lips curled upwards in a primitive expression of overwhelming lust. Megan's breasts swelled and now the caress of her fingers through the material of her panties was no longer enough. She could tell that both Leonora and Renato were about to climax and suddenly the ache between her thighs had to be assuaged. She slid her fingers inside the leg of the panties, pushed aside her swollen sex lips and began to rub the area around her throbbing clitoris.

Out in the garden Leonora's tiny fists began to beat on her lover's chest and then the pair of them were shuddering in an ecstatic climax, a climax that was swiftly followed by Megan's as she masturbated herself to blissful release and felt the hot warmth spread through her lower body, while her juices flowed copiously. She trembled from head to foot, her cheeks flushed and hot, ashamed of what she'd done and yet excited by all that she'd witnessed.

'How's it going?' asked Fabrizio from the doorway.

With a gasp Megan dropped her skirt and turned to face him. Her breathing was rapid and she felt certain that he must know what she'd been doing, but his face was expressionless and after a few seconds she decided that she was wrong. 'Fine,' she said nervously, her voice slightly shaky.

'Admiring the view?' he enquired, crossing the room to stand beside her.

Megan was horribly aware of the faintly musky smell of sex that surrounded her. 'I was looking at your sister,' she confessed. 'That's a lovely horse she rides.'

Fabrizio stared out of the window. 'I can't see a horse, or Leonora come to that.'

'They were there a minute ago,' Megan assured him.

'I didn't think you'd imagined it,' he said sardonically. 'I really came to see if you wanted a cup of coffee.'

Megan's legs felt so weak that she thought she'd fall down if she didn't sit. 'That would be lovely,' she admitted.

Fabrizio rested an arm lightly round her shoulders. 'After lunch, before you start work again, I must show you round the grounds. I don't want you locked away here with nothing to look at except these dusty old books.'

There was something in his voice that made Megan wonder if he did know after all, if he had witnessed everything that she'd seen and done, but that thought was impossible to bear and she pushed it hastily away. 'I'd like that.'

'I'll have your coffee sent in. Have you discovered any rare treasures yet?' He gestured towards the piles of books.

'One or two,' she admitted. 'I need to get hold of a first editions guide so that I can be certain how much they're worth. It will make a difference to your insurance.'

'How thoughtful of you to think about my insurance,' said Fabrizio. He looked consideringly at her. 'Your colour's better now. You were quite pale at breakfast.'

Megan felt mortified. 'I'm enjoying what I'm doing.'

'Yes,' he said slowly. 'I rather thought you were.' And with that he left the room, and Megan began to think that he definitely knew what she'd been doing. The trouble was, she had no idea how long he'd been standing in the doorway. If he'd been there a few minutes then he would obviously have realised, and that thought was so mortifying that she wanted to run from the house.

It wasn't as though it was like her. She'd never done anything remotely similar in her life before. It was simply that Leonora and Renato's need had been so urgent, so all-powerful, that it had aroused desire in Megan, desire of an intensity she'd never known before. She supposed that part of it was due to the fact that she found Fabrizio so attractive, but that was no excuse. However, even though she was ashamed she had a feeling that here, in this strange household, what she'd done would not be considered as outrageous or abnormal as it would at home in Lincolnshire.

Much to Megan's disappointment there was no sign of Fabrizio at lunch, and she joined Leonora and Alessandra for a simple but delicious meal of Parma ham, assorted cheeses, crusty bread and a tossed green salad with a choice of exotic fresh fruits to follow. Both girls asked her questions about the library and seemed genuinely interested in her replies, but whenever Megan spoke to Leonora she was distracted by the memory of what she'd seen the blonde girl doing with Renato earlier that morning.

Just as she finished eating and was about to return to the library, Fabrizio came into the room. 'Good, I've caught you. I've come to fulfil my promise to show you the grounds before you return to work.'

'Shall I come with you?' asked Alessandra.

'There's no need,' said Fabrizio dismissively, and Megan saw a slight frown cross his girlfriend's face. She could understand it, but she was also pleased. It meant that she could pretend for a brief moment that she and Fabrizio were a couple, and that his attentions were due to desire and not the simple politeness of a courteous employer.

As she'd expected the grounds were magnificent; immaculate lawns surrounded by flowering shrubs and bushes, while at the far end of the lawns, just before reaching a small copse that was also part of the grounds, there was a beautiful lake. Fabrizio caught hold of Megan's hand and led her to the edge. 'Somewhere within the lake there is a large trout,' he explained. 'I myself have only seen him once, the others never. My uncle was very proud of him because he had watched him grow from a tiny fish. He, like me, took pleasure from watching things expand and blossom into their full beauty.'

As he spoke he turned Megan towards him and started to run his fingers through her curly hair, piling it up on the top of her head for a moment before releasing it again. 'You must never cut your hair,' he said softly. 'It's beautiful.'

Megan wasn't used to compliments and didn't know how to cope. 'I think it's a bit old-fashioned.'

He shook his head. 'For me it's a sign that you are not what you would have people believe. The way it tumbles and falls, free and natural, that, I believe, is the true you. You wear sensible clothes that conceal a lovely figure,' and here he flicked a dismissive finger at her blouse, 'and you do not move well but these are minor things. It is your hair that tells me the truth about you, Megan.'

'What is the truth?' she whispered, staring up at him.

'That is something I will show you in time,' he promised her.

'You don't know me at all,' she protested.

'I think it's possible that I know you better than you know yourself. Why are you blushing?'

'Am I?' She put her hands to her cheeks. They were hot, but that was because she was remembering the way she'd behaved that morning. She was embarrassed by that, rather than by what he was saying. 'It's very warm here,' she said lamely.

'Then we'll move on to the copse. The trees there will shade us from the sun.'

Megan hesitated. Suddenly she was afraid to go into the woods with him. She was too attracted to him, and too afraid of making a fool of herself if he touched her again. For all she knew this was the way Italian men behaved. It might mean very little to him, but to her the feel of his fingers in her hair had sent her blood racing. If she over-reacted he might be embarrassed, feel that he had to ask her to leave and that would be unbearable. But even if she was right and he was flirting with her, she wasn't ready to cope with the intensity of passion that she suspected he'd bring to a relationship.

'I think it's time I went back now,' she said crisply. 'You're not paying me to waste my time walking in the woods.'

'I'm paying you to do what I ask,' he retorted.

Megan stared at him. 'That isn't true.'

'It is. It seems you didn't read your contract very carefully.'

'I'm here to catalogue the library, that's what it said in the advert.'

He gave a half smile. 'But not in the contract. In the contract it said that you were here to help me in the library and in any other way that proved necessary.'

'I saw that, but I thought you meant necessary in order to get the library straight.'

'That's not what it said, was it?' he asked.

'No, but ... ' Megan didn't know what to say.

Fabrizio's hands gripped her shoulders tightly and she felt herself start to sway towards him. 'You have so much to learn,' he whispered. 'And I will teach you it all. You will be so thankful that you came here, so grateful for everything that you are taught. You're not afraid are you?' Abruptly his hands released her and Megan swayed a little on her feet.

'Why should I be afraid?' she asked, trying hard to sound brisk and efficient. 'You're not going to hurt me are you?'

Fabrizio looked at her thoughtfully. 'That rather depends on what you mean by "hurt".'

Looking into his dark, dangerously sexy eyes Megan realised that she should be afraid, very afraid, but when he'd touched her he'd changed her. She felt like a different woman, suddenly aware that she had the potential to be sensual and sexy. It was a liberating feeling and as a result she dismissed the warning note from her brain. Maybe this man was dangerous. Perhaps living here was going to prove a painful experience. Nevertheless, she would do anything, anything at all for the chance to go to bed with Fabrizio.

'Whatever I mean by it, I want to get back to work now,' she said firmly and before he could say anything more she turned and began to walk back to the house. As she walked she swayed her hips a little more than usual, quite unconsciously becoming more sensual, more provocative in the way she moved. Standing by the lake watching her, Fabrizio gave a small smile of satisfaction. Renato was quite wrong, he thought to himself. Megan was going to be an excellent pupil.

Chapter Five

The days of the week flew past for Megan, partly because her work was extremely demanding, but also because she was becoming increasingly attracted to Fabrizio. After their walk in the grounds, when he'd touched her hair, he'd continued to spend some time with her every day. And whenever they were alone she would wait, her nerves tense with anticipation, for him to touch her, which he never failed to do.

Sometimes he would merely put an arm around her waist for a few seconds; at other times he'd run his fingers through her hair or smooth her back with the palm of his hand. Whatever he did the result on Megan was always electrifying, until by the time her first weekend in Sussex arrived she was thoroughly frustrated, unable to be sure that these touches meant as much to him as they did to her.

When she went down to breakfast on the Saturday morning there was no one in the dining room, and for the first time she ate alone. As she was finishing, Fabrizio came in. 'What are you planning to do today?'

'Work in the library, of course.'

'I don't expect you to keep yourself locked away seven days a week you know. Weekends are for leisure activities.'

'I don't mind,' Megan assured him. 'The work's fascinating and soon I'll ...'

'I'll take you for a drive,' Fabrizio announced. 'Do you have a scarf that you can tie over your hair? It gets windy with the top down. I trust you enjoy being driven fast?'

'I don't know,' admitted Megan. 'I'm a very careful driver myself, and Nick's car was too old to go fast.'

'Then we will find out.'

Fifteen minutes later Megan was sitting next to him in the car. She was already nervous, not because he was going to drive fast but because they were so close. She could smell the light lemony tang of his aftershave, and as the day was warm he was wearing a short-sleeved shirt. For the first time she saw his muscular forearms with their fine covering of dark hairs. As he started the car she noticed his fingers, long and sensitive, and wondered what it would feel like to have them touch her intimately.

'Seat belt fastened?' he asked briskly, and without waiting for an answer proceeded to speed down the drive and out into the road.

The next hour was one of the most terrifying of Megan's life. Although they were never in danger of having an accident, the sheer speed of the car, coupled with the rushing sensation of the wind in her face, made it seem as though she was flying rather than being driven. Fabrizio seemed to hate having any car in front of him, seeing it as a challenge to be overtaken. Eventually he took a sharp turning to the left and slowed as they entered a tiny village. 'There's a good pub here, we can have coffee. How are you enjoying yourself?'

Megan unclenched her fingers. 'I'm not certain that I *am* enjoying myself.'

'You should learn to relax more,' he said lightly.

Over coffee he questioned Megan closely about her

family and friends. They were both resting their elbows on the table, which was so small that their arms were almost touching. Megan wished that they were, or that he'd suddenly take her hand and kiss her fingertips, as Franco had kissed them on the night she arrived. She couldn't understand why she'd started having these thoughts. No other man had ever had this effect on her, certainly not Nick.

'Do you always watch people so intensely?' enquired Fabrizio. 'It's quite unsettling.'

Megan gave an awkward laugh. 'I'm sorry, I was miles away.'

'That's a pity. I hoped you were thinking about me.'

She blushed, grateful that he didn't know the truth. 'You haven't told me anything about yourself,' she replied.

'There's really nothing in my past that would interest you.'

'How do you know that?'

'Because you wouldn't understand the kind of life I've led. Shall we continue driving and stop somewhere for lunch or would you rather go back to the house? I'm afraid the others have gone out for the day so whatever you choose you'll only have me for company.'

Megan stared at him. 'Where have they gone?'

'Shopping. I draw the line at shopping, which is why Franco's had to go to carry Alessandra's parcels for her. Renato doesn't seem to mind. Of course it's different for him, he isn't paying for Leonora's purchases. When I'm with Alessandra I'm wondering if I'm going to have to sell the family business in order to keep her in clothes.' He laughed.

'I don't mind what we do,' confessed Megan.

'Are you sure?' he asked intently.

Megan's heart began to race. She was virtually certain that he was propositioning her, that if they went back to the house he was going to do more than just touch her arm or her hair, but she still couldn't understand why he was attracted to her when he had a girlfriend like Alessandra.

She knew that she should say she wanted a pub lunch, that would be safe and sensible. If they went back to the house and anything happened, the situation would become awkward. He was her employer, and Alessandra had been very friendly towards her.

Her tingling flesh helped her to put her scruples to one side. After all, it was Fabrizio who was forever telling her that she must learn to live life to the full. At least this way she would find out whether she was right, whether he was attracted to her.

'Quite sure,' she said, looking him straight in the eye.

Quickly he got to his feet and his fingers circled her wrist. 'We'll go back to the house,' he said firmly.

If anything he drove even faster on the return journey, but this time Megan felt exhilarated. She had confidence in him as a driver and was beginning to enjoy the sensation of speed. When they drew up outside the house she looked at him and laughed. 'That time I did enjoy it.'

He nodded. 'So, you need to experience things twice in order to understand that they can give you pleasure?'

'Not always, but in this case yes.'

'I must remember that.'

For a moment she was afraid to go into the house with him. His words were so strange, carrying undertones that she didn't like to dwell on, but then his expression lightened and he took hold of her hand. 'Come, now I will try and give you more pleasure.'

As soon as they were inside the front door Fabrizio caught Megan in his arms and began to kiss her. At first his kisses were slow and languorous, but as his passion mounted his mouth became more demanding, his tongue invading her mouth, and she responded with equal urgency.

'Let's go upstairs,' he whispered huskily, and looked at Megan to see her reaction. She could hardly believe that this was happening but nodded shyly, desperate now to lie naked with him and feel his skin against hers.

They hurried up the stairs to the second floor but Fabrizio guided her past her bedroom door and on to the next room. 'We will be private here, no risk of the servants overhearing you,' he said with a smile.

The room was similar to Megan's bedroom but the bed was smaller and against the wall, leaving a bigger space in the middle of the room. Fabrizio's first action was to draw the heavy drapes across the window, blocking out the sunlight. Then he flicked a switch so that three spotlights came on. 'That's better, much better,' he murmured.

Megan didn't know why it was better. She thought it would be rather nice to lie on the bed and look out of the window, but by shutting out the light Fabrizio had changed the atmosphere in the room. This was certainly more erotic, yet it also made her feel more vulnerable.

A large, full-length mirror was set in the wall opposite the bed and Fabrizio guided Megan until she was standing in front of it. She stared at her own reflection and watched him as he stood behind her, put his hands round her waist and then bent his head to nuzzle at the delicate skin behind her right ear. 'You don't know how much I've longed for this moment,' he whispered, his teeth nibbling her earlobe. Her skin prickled and she was weak with desire. 'I want you to undress for me,' he continued.

Megan stared at him in the mirror, her eyes wide with surprise, and Fabrizio's face looked impassively back at her. Suddenly she felt gauche, like a schoolgirl on her first date. She'd expected him to undress her, probably quickly and with an efficiency born out of years of practice. 'I don't know how to start,' she said shyly.

'Of course you do. I want you to watch yourself in the mirror as you strip, and watch my face as well. Don't speak at all. I prefer silence at the beginning.'

Megan began to tremble, partly out of desire and partly out of fear. She'd never experienced anything like this before and didn't know how to respond. The only thing she did know was that she wanted this man more than she'd ever wanted anyone and, as a result, she must push her inhibitions to one side.

As she continued to gaze into the mirror, her figure caught in one of the spotlights, her fingers fumbled with the buttons of her blouse. She half expected him to remove it from her shoulders once it was unfastened but he remained behind her, his eyes always watching her. After shrugging off the blouse she unzipped her linen skirt and stepped out of it. Beneath it she was wearing flesh-coloured tights and she saw Fabrizio frown. She looked enquiringly at him but he didn't speak, simply gestured for her to continue. She started to bend forward to take her tights off and immediately he placed a hand on her shoulder.

'Remove your bra first,' he said quietly.

Megan didn't want to remove her bra; she didn't want to see her embarrassingly large breasts spill out, but his words brooked no argument. Reaching behind her she undid the clasp, shrugged the straps off her shoulders and leant forward a little to let the garment fall to the floor before straightening up.

Fabrizio gave a small sigh of contentment. 'You have magnificent breasts. I had no idea. You've always kept them so well covered.'

Megan knew she wasn't expected to answer him. Now, as she bent forward from the waist to remove her tights, her breasts hung down. They felt bigger than usual, swelling with excitement, and she could feel her nipples prickling. When it came to removing her panties she hesitated awkwardly, looking appealingly at Fabrizio in the mirror in the hope that he'd do this for her, but he was still watching her closely and she got no response. Hastily she pulled them down and stepped out of them.

'Now stand up straight and look at yourself,' he instructed. 'See how beautiful your body is, how soft and feminine.'

Megan swallowed hard. She'd never had enough confidence in herself to stand naked in front of a mirror and examine every inch of her body. Even now she didn't like what she saw. She seemed ridiculously top heavy with her slim hips and full breasts, but obviously Fabrizio didn't feel the same about her.

He turned her a little so that she could no longer see her reflection but, unknown to her, Leonora, Renato, Alessandra and Franco could all see her very well from behind the two-way mirror, as Fabrizio had intended all along.

It only took him a few seconds to strip off his own clothes, which he left in a heap on the floor before reaching out and touching each of Megan's breasts lightly with his fingers. Instantly her nipples sprang fully erect and to her delight he lowered his head and kissed each of them in turn, rolling his tongue in lazy circles around the areolae and then drawing the tight little peaks into his mouth one after the other, sucking harder than Nick had ever done and causing electric flashes to streak through her from breast to belly.

Gradually he sank to his knees in front of her, his mouth and tongue caressing the flesh over her ribs and belly before he parted her legs and she felt his tongue separating her sex lips. She quivered with delight as the tip of his tongue lapped at her juices.

'You taste delicious,' he said huskily, lifting his head for a moment. 'Here, taste yourself.' Getting to his feet he kissed her on the mouth, pushing his tongue into hers.

She was shocked; she'd never dreamt that people did things like this, but she was also incredibly aroused. She moaned softly and immediately Fabrizio picked her up and carried her over to the bed. Lying on her back she looked up at him, her eyes wide, the pupils dilated with passion. Giving a half smile he nodded to himself and Megan wondered what he was thinking.

She was aching between her thighs where his mouth had been and her hips began to twitch on the bed as she was consumed with a need for the stimulation to continue. Fabrizio watched her for a few moments and then slid a hand between her thighs. At last his long, lean fingers were manipulating her flesh, touching her where she so desperately needed to be touched, and at the same time his mouth was moving from one breast to the other.

She felt as though her skin was melting and her moans grew louder. The wonderful hot warmth of impending orgasm rushed through her lower belly and between her thighs. Her back arched off the bed and as his fingers gripped the stem of her clitoris, pressing firmly on it, so his teeth grazed the tip of her left nipple. These two sensations caused her body to spasm violently and she gave a cry of delight.

As the last ripples of her contraction died away she waited for him to enter her, but instead he moved an armchair into the centre of the room, its back towards the mirror. Without a word he pushed Megan into a kneeling position on the seat of the chair with her arms resting on the top of the back, her voluptuous breasts balanced between them. The fabric covering the arm-chair was slightly rough in texture and her nipples sprang instantly erect as they rubbed against it. Fabrizio spread her legs wide so that they were resting against the sides of the chair and then he knelt facing her back, his knees balanced on the front of the seat, and his hands pulled her hips towards him before moving round her ribcage so that his thumbs could touch the undersides of her breasts.

She was so wet and aroused that it was easy for him to penetrate her from behind, and as she felt the tip of him slide inside her she began to shudder as yet another delicious wave of pleasure rushed through her. She watched herself in the mirror, unable to believe that this was happening. As Fabrizio began to thrust inside her, her breasts were pushed back and forth until they were so swollen and aching that she longed for them to be touched, but Fabrizio's hands were busy stroking her belly and gradually moving even lower.

She desperately wanted to feel his fingers between her sex lips again and so without thinking she began to massage her own breasts, uttering throaty little cries as she fingered her rigid nipples and kneaded her full breasts.

'That's right,' whispered Fabrizio. 'Give yourself all the pleasure you can. Here in this house life is about nothing but pleasure.'

She could feel the pressure deepening inside her, feel the hot liquid excitement getting ready to rush through her, and whimpered frantically as her clitoris throbbed in lonely isolation. Finally, when she was ready to scream with frustration, Fabrizio's fingers located the flesh around the tightly bunched collection of nerve endings. At last every part of her was being stimulated, every part pulsating with pleasure. Her swollen breasts and erect nipples, her gently rounded belly, her throbbing clitoris, all of them were being manipulated to give her maximum excitement. At the same time Fabrizio moved in and out of her, his tempo now hard and fast.

'You're nearly there,' Fabrizio said huskily. 'See if you can hold back, make it last a little longer.'

She wanted to because it all felt so wonderful, but any chance she'd had of delaying it was ruined by his words, and by the fact that his fingers were pressing so knowingly between her thighs as he drove towards his own climax. The sight of the pair of them in the mirror was the final trigger for Megan and as she pinched at her nipples she felt her stomach muscles slither and shift in preparation for release.

'I'm coming!' she cried helplessly, and within seconds her body was racked by pleasure.

'Too soon,' groaned Fabrizio, but as her internal muscles spasmed helplessly around his swollen cock, she saw his head go back and then felt him shuddering against her until all the tension had drained out of him and he slumped on her back, his breath warm against the nape of her neck.

Megan was still riveted by their reflection in the mirror. Her long curls were tumbling around her face, falling forward and tickling her breasts where they were balanced on the back of the chair. Her lips looked moist, her cheeks flushed and her eyes bright. She'd never felt so relaxed or so satisfied, and the sound of their rapid breathing filling the room only emphasised the pleasure he'd just given her. She gave a tiny smile of happiness.

'She certainly enjoyed that,' said Renato, sitting on a chair in the next room. He, along with the others, had watched the entire seduction with keen interest.

'Of course she did, he made sure of that,' said Alessandra irritably. 'She won't be smiling quite so much in a few days' time.'

'You don't sound very happy,' laughed Leonora. 'He did warn you that he'd have to gain her confidence before we could begin the games. I must say, she was much more sexy than I'd expected, don't you agree Renato?'

'She was very responsive,' he said neutrally.

'I thought they both looked as though they had a good time,' continued Leonora, and she heard Franco muffle a laugh.

'It's all right for you three, but it wasn't very nice for me,' Alessandra pointed out. 'I wish I hadn't watched.'

'You had to watch,' said Leonora. 'At least now you know some of the things she likes.'

'I'm more interested in the things she won't like.'

'There's plenty of time for all that,' Renato assured her. 'Fabrizio was probably bored stiff today.'

'He was certainly stiff,' said Leonora with a mischievous smile. 'I thought he was having quite a good time.'

'Why are you trying to upset me?' asked Alessandra.

'Because then you'll be all the more determined to

make her suffer,' said Leonora. 'You're nicer than I am, Alessandra. Without watching this you'd probably have felt sorry for her as soon as the games began in earnest.'

'Perhaps I would have done, but I certainly don't now.'

'Which is precisely what Fabrizio intended,' Renato pointed out.

'And when do we start to teach her our ways?' asked Franco.

Renato stood up, trying to adjust himself so that the others couldn't see how turned on he'd been by it all. 'Soon,' he promised Franco. 'Certainly within the next few days.'

'How wonderful!' enthused Leonora, slipping her arm through Alessandra's. 'Come on, let's go shopping. And don't worry, that's the last time Megan Stewart will look quite so satisfied for a very long time.'

Chapter Six

For the next three nights Fabrizio came to Megan's room, where he devoted himself entirely to giving her seemingly endless hours of pleasure. Until now she'd never believed the stories she'd read about multi-orgasmic women, and she was amazed at how many climaxes he coaxed from her. Fabrizio's sole aim seemed to be to bring her body alive, watching her closely as she moaned and writhed, swamped by wave after wave of delicious ecstasy.

On the Wednesday night she waited as usual for him to come to her, but he didn't appear. She was stunned. He hadn't said anything the night before to suggest it was over. If anything she'd felt that they'd been closer than at any other time. The trouble was, there was nothing she could do. She could hardly go running down the stairs and knock on the door of the bedroom that he shared with Alessandra, asking him why he wasn't with her.

All the time he had been with her she'd wondered what Alessandra must be thinking, but assumed that he'd invented some story which had satisfied his beautiful lover. Perhaps now Alessandra had guessed what had been happening. If so, Megan didn't know how she'd bear it.

Lying restlessly in her bed she let her hands wander over her body, pretending that they were Fabrizio's hands. She ran the back of her fingers over her hipbones, and parted her thighs so that they could wander idly between them. Thinking of Fabrizio she was quickly damp, but although she had a small climax it was so different from the intensity of the orgasms that he himself had given her that she stopped. There didn't seem any point. She needed him, and his skilful lovemaking, to achieve full satisfaction. By spending so many hours with her he'd spoilt the small, solitary pleasure of masturbation.

When he came into the library the following

morning she waited for him to say something, to explain his absence from her bed, but he behaved as though nothing had ever happened between them. They talked about the books and various ways of cataloguing them and then he turned to leave. Unable to bear it Megan heard herself call out his name. 'Fabrizio!'

Turning his head he looked questioningly at her. 'Something's wrong?'

She didn't know what to say. 'It's only that ... I missed you last night.'

'I see. I'm afraid I'm a busy man. It may be that I will not be able to visit you again.'

'Not ever?' she asked in horror.

'Perhaps not. But it was good for you, yes?'

'Of course it was good,' she whispered. 'You must know that.'

For the first time he smiled. 'Yes, I could hardly fail to tell.'

'You've made me need you,' she muttered.

'Excuse me?'

'You've made me need you,' she said more loudly, thoroughly ashamed of herself but desperate that he should understand.

'As I told you, life here is all about pleasure. I wanted you to experience some as well.'

'I don't want it to end,' she blurted out.

Fabrizio raised his eyebrows. 'I see. In that case meet me in the top floor second bedroom, at ten o'clock tomorrow evening. I will be waiting there for you.'

'I've got to go into town tomorrow evening. I'm meeting the antique books specialist for dinner, have you forgotten?'

'Yes, I had forgotten,' he said smoothly. 'It's of no matter, you will be back by ten.'

'Why can't you come to my room?' asked Megan.

'I'm bored with coming to your room. I want a change. It's time for us to do something different.'

Megan's heart raced. 'You can't come to me tonight?' She hated herself for begging but her body was desperate for the satisfaction that he'd taught it to expect.

'Regretfully no,' he said crisply, and with that he was gone.

Fabrizio and the others were sitting outside in the garden as Megan continued to work in the library. 'She's ready for the next stage,' he announced. 'It's as I'd hoped. Her flesh is so used to pleasure that she cannot bear to be without it.'

'But will she be desperate enough to go along with what you have in mind?' asked Alessandra.

'Of course she will,' said Leonora. 'Imagine what it must be like to learn what sex is really about for the first time and then have the pleasure taken away from you. By tomorrow night she'll do anything for an orgasm.'

'Perhaps not anything,' said Fabrizio, 'but certainly she won't turn and run the moment she enters the room.'

'What if she does?' asked Renato.

'Then I will starve her body for a little longer. Since she cannot leave the house very often she will have to stay here, watching and listening to the rest of us as we kiss and caress in front of her. She is trapped. There is only one way for her to go, and that is forward.'

'I expect you're glad his private sessions with her are over, Alessandra?' said Renato. 'It must have been difficult for you.'

'Alessandra understands that they were necessary,' snapped Fabrizio.

'Would you be as understanding, Leonora?' asked Franco.

Leonora frowned. 'You mean if Renato did the same

thing?' Franco nodded. 'Yes, I think so. I'd be so excited at the thought of what was going to happen in the future that it would be worth any feelings of jealousy.'

'You don't have a jealous bone in your body,' said Renato. 'Your emotions don't run deep enough for jealousy.'

'They do,' Leonora protested. 'You make me sound shallow and I'm not.'

'You're a very strong woman, Leonora,' said Franco admiringly. 'Perhaps Renato has that confused with lack of feeling.'

'Why don't you mind your own business,' suggested Renato sharply.

Franco shrugged. 'As you wish. I wonder what Leonora would do if she met a man as strong as herself.'

'Ignore him,' said Renato. Then to Franco, 'Leonora doesn't like weak men; she likes men whose sexuality complements her own. I doubt you fit that criteria.'

Fabrizio, who'd been listening carefully, leant forward in his chair. 'It doesn't matter whether he does or he doesn't. I would never countenance a relationship between Franco and Leonora, as they both know very well.'

'You don't own me,' retorted Leonora.

'I'm the head of the family, and I also control the purse strings,' Fabrizio reminded her. Leonora regarded him sulkily.

'About Megan,' said Alessandra, anxious to lighten the mood. 'What exactly do you have planned for tomorrow night?'

'Tomorrow night will be a slow introduction to our ways,' said Fabrizio. 'I shall only need you in attendance, Alessandra.' He glanced at the other three. 'I know you're disappointed but if we rush things now we spoil everything. You must trust me in this.'

'Can we watch through the mirror again?' asked Leonora eagerly.

Fabrizio shook his head. 'I think not. I don't wish you to know too much about her body's responses. Believe me, it will be more interesting done my way. You have only a few more days to wait and then you too will be involved.'

'I'm turned on already,' announced Leonora. She went and sat on Renato's lap, her hand unzipping his fly, and reaching inside she began to fondle him. 'You're excited too,' she said gleefully. 'Let's take the horses out and we can make love somewhere in the countryside.'

121

'Remember to take your whip, Leonora,' drawled Franco.

Renato shot the other man an angry glance. 'Why don't you find a girlfriend of your own instead of prying into our sex life,' he demanded.

Fabrizio watched his sister and her lover depart and then looked thoughtfully at his secretary. 'I think Renato has made a very good point. Although from time to time you join in our games, you must remember that your position here is that of an employee.'

'You mean I'm like the English girl?'

'Hardly, but neither are you like Renato. It may be a difficult situation for you to be in but if you don't like it then you need not stay.'

Franco got to his feet. 'You can't control everyone's lives all the time you know. I must get to work. See to some of those letters you dictated this morning. I hope it goes well for you tomorrow night. I believe you said I will be called on to participate in Megan's seduction at some stage.'

'Naturally. Every one of us will be involved.'

'Excellent. Then please excuse me, I'll return to work.'

Alone in the garden Fabrizio closed his eyes and lifted his face to the sun. It was one of the things he missed most, living here in England for six months. So many of the days were overcast, or spoilt by a cool breeze but today was perfect; even more so because of the prospect of the following night.

Megan tapped hesitantly on the bedroom door. She'd thought the evening with the antique book dealer would never end and had driven back to the Sussex house as fast as she could, her flesh already throbbing in anticipation of the pleasures that awaited it. She only hoped that Fabrizio hadn't lost patience and decided not to wait for her. To her relief the door was instantly opened and he drew her inside, but when he closed it he turned the key in the lock.

'Why are you doing that?' she asked nervously.

'We don't want to be disturbed do we?'

The room was very dark, so dark that she could scarcely make out where the bed was. 'Aren't you going to put on the lights?'

'Not yet. Don't you find the darkness exciting?' As he spoke he began to undress her, unzipping the back of her dress and removing her bra before peeling down the hold-up stockings that he'd encouraged her to wear. Within seconds she was left in the silk panties she'd bought that very afternoon.

'Nice,' he said appreciatively, running his hand over the fabric. 'Much sexier than your usual sensible cotton.' She was trembling with desire, and there was a tightness in her lower belly, a tightness borne out of expectation of the sensual gratification that he'd soon grant her. 'I want to keep you in darkness tonight,' he whispered, running his hands through her hair and gently massaging her scalp.

Megan sighed with pleasure but at the same time her senses grew alert to the possibility of danger. 'What do you mean?'

His reply was to place his hands around her face and suddenly her eyes were covered by a thick velvet band that fitted snugly over the bridge of her nose. 'No!' she protested.

'It will increase the pleasure,' he promised her. His hands fondled her breasts, full and heavy, the nipples painfully hard. 'See how ready you are. Surely you don't want me to stop now?'

'No,' she whispered.

She felt his fingers at her hips and then he was

pushing the leg of her panties to one side, his tongue licking the creases at the tops of her thighs, but although she pushed her hips forward he didn't allow it to stray where she most wanted it to go. She felt his teeth nip at her tender flesh and uttered a tiny squeal of protest which he ignored. Taking her hands he led her across the room and she found that she was pulling back, afraid of the darkness.

'Don't be silly, Megan,' he said calmly. 'You've been in this room plenty of times. There's nothing here to frighten you.'

'I feel strange like this.'

'That's the whole idea. Without sight your other senses will work harder, which will increase your pleasure. Trust me.'

He sat her on the edge of the bed and then he moved away for a moment, leaving her feeling horribly isolated. Within seconds he'd returned and to her surprise started binding her heavy breasts with what felt like a kind of muslin strip. He tied it tightly, squashing her breasts against her ribcage and again she gave a moan of protest, because the constriction made her engorged breasts ache even more.

'Lie on your back,' he commanded.

'I don't like this,' she whimpered. 'Please take the blindfold off.'

'If I take the blindfold off then the evening is finished.'

Megan fell silent. Her body was screaming for satisfaction, there was no way she could let him stop now. Trembling from head to foot she lay on her back, staring into the blackness and feeling the pressure of the muslin material. When Fabrizio's warm hands caressed her ribcage she started to relax, but then, with shocking abruptness, cold liquid was poured on to the muslin and she cried out. 'What are you doing?'

'Relax, *cara*,' he murmured. 'Enjoy these different sensations.'

'But it's cold.'

He ran the backs of his fingers over the thin material, feeling the sharp pointed tips of her nipples. 'Don't deny you're excited by it.'

She couldn't understand how it had happened. She could have sworn that both Fabrizio's hands had been on her when the cold liquid had flowed over her breasts, but even as she tried to work out what he'd done his lips were fastening around each of the cold, constricted nipples in turn. He blew on them, his breath warm in total contrast to the earlier chill. It was delicious and her breasts began to swell, but their growth was limited by the tightness of the muslin and as, a result they started to throb and ache, so that the sensation was more pain than pleasure.

She squirmed frantically beneath his mouth. 'What's the matter?' he asked.

'My breasts are aching,' she confessed.

'Doesn't it feel good? When I suck on your nipples like this, isn't it nice?' He began to suck hard and shards of pleasure mingled with the pain to create an extraordinary sensation that set her lower body squirming restlessly. She wanted to feel him inside her, needed something to ease the hollow, aching sensation between her thighs, but he showed no interest in entering her yet. Gradually his breath and careful sucking and nibbling warmed her breasts until she was able to relax again.

'That's better,' he murmured and his hands circled her waist, pressing inwards which caused an ache to start above her pubic bone. His fingers were splayed out over her flesh. She could picture how they must look so clearly that for a moment she thought she must be imagining it when a third hand brushed softly between her thighs, tracing a delicate path between her sex lips, gliding along the damp channel and touching the side of her clitoris in an exquisite caress that made her lower body arch off the bed in delight.

'Who's doing that?' she cried, as the hand continued its knowing arousal of her shamefully willing flesh. 'Fabrizio, I don't like this. Who's here with us?'

'It's only Alessandra,' he murmured. 'She's your friend, and wants to give you pleasure, too.'

'No!' exclaimed Megan. 'I don't want her here.'

'I want her here if I'm to continue,' said Fabrizio coldly. 'Do you wish us both to leave?'

Megan continued to tremble violently and now, to add to her confusion, cold water was again trickled on to her bandaged breasts, causing them to throb once more. This only served to increase the aching lower down, which Alessandra's fingers were about to satisfy. 'I don't know what I want,' she sobbed, and in response Alessandra swirled a finger around Megan's clitoris and her body spasmed violently as a climax tore through her.

'Excellent,' said Fabrizio. 'Very well done, Alessandra. How damp is she?' Megan was mortified to hear them discuss her like this, yet it was also horribly arousing. She was glad now that she was blindfolded, that she wasn't able to see what they were doing to her wanton body.

'She's very damp,' replied Alessandra, sliding three fingers inside Megan and moving them gently around her entrance. Megan gasped as flickers of arousal seared through her.

'Then use one of the marble dildos on her,' said Fabrizio.

Megan froze in shock. The words were terrifying and she began to protest, but any arguments were muffled when Fabrizio's mouth covered hers. At last his hands began to remove the freezing cloth that was binding her needy breasts. When they were finally free he stopped kissing her lips and moved his mouth to them instead. He rubbed his face against the undersides of each in turn, and she felt the slight roughness of his stubble grazing the tender skin. She loved the feeling and sighed with contentment.

Even as she sighed and relaxed, her thighs were pushed apart by Alessandra and now she felt something hard, smooth and cold being eased inside her. Her body stiffened. 'That's too big,' she whispered.

'Nonsense, it's the smallest size there is. You need to

relax more that's all,' retorted Fabrizio. Megan tried to obey but she couldn't take her mind off what was happening to her, and whimpered as the steady, insidious pressure continued to mount.

'I think she needs distracting,' said Alessandra.

Megan could hear herself uttering tiny sobs, a mixture of fear and need. She couldn't believe that this was happening to her, that she was allowing a man and a woman to use her body in this shameful way, and yet her nerve endings were more alive than ever before. She sensed that if she could only go along with what they were doing she would experience greater pleasure than she had ever known.

Fabrizio didn't answer his mistress and Megan waited for him to touch her in one of the ways he knew she liked best, to distract her with his mouth or lips. She was surprised. With shocking abruptness she felt something strike her across her unprotected abdomen. It felt like a whip, and a red-hot burning sensation filled her belly. Her scream of shock echoed around the room.

'It will lead to pleasure,' Fabrizio murmured to her as he used the cool tip of his tongue to lick along the path where the whip had fallen. The sensations were so different, so overwhelming, that her whole body shook and she completely forgot about Alessandra. All at once the violet-eyed girl twisted and pushed the dildo forcefully inside Megan; at the same time her fingers stroked the shaft of Megan's clitoris.

Megan stopped resisting. There was nothing she could do except allow these two to have their way with her. As she allowed all the sensations to flood through her, her body was shattered by an almost painful orgasm that tore through her every fibre, and her body thrashed around on the bed. Alessandra and Fabrizio quickly grabbed hold of her to keep her from falling.

As the final spasms died away she let out a sigh.

'You see, I promised you even greater pleasure,' said Fabrizio. 'I think one more and then we will finish for the night.'

'No, I can't come again,' Megan protested.

'Of course you can.'

Megan gave a cry as the marble column was pulled swiftly out of her, and then the tip was eased back inside her again. This time Alessandra rotated it as she inserted it, touching the walls of Megan's vagina and stimulating even more nerve endings. The strange, heavy pressure began to increase, a pulse throbbed deep inside Megan, somewhere behind her clitoris, and her body began to stiffen.

'She's nearly there,' murmured Fabrizio, and as Megan's head pressed back against the pillow he delivered another stinging blow across her belly. This time she hardly noticed the pain because it only added an edge to her pleasure, an edge that was enough to push her into yet another glorious climax where pleasure and pain joined together in an incredible combination, leaving her utterly ashamed of the way she'd responded, yet more satisfied than ever before.

No more words were spoken. She heard the door open and close and as Fabrizio removed her blindfold and pulled her to her feet, she realised that Alessandra had departed. She felt weak and shaky and hoped for some gesture of tenderness from him, but all he did was hand her her clothes. 'Get dressed,' he said curtly. 'It's time for us to sleep now.'

'I didn't know it could be like this,' she murmured.

His fingers touched her lightly under the chin. 'Believe me, little one, this was nothing at all.'

Leonora made sure that she was down for breakfast in good time the following morning. Having been deprived of the chance of watching Megan take her first tentative steps into Fabrizio's world of debauchery she was anxious to see for herself how the English girl looked the following morning. Much to her disappointment there was no sign of Megan, only Alessandra was at the breakfast table.

'How did it go?' Leonora asked eagerly.

'It was interesting,' said Alessandra, toying with a piece of toast.

'What do you mean interesting? Did she resist?'

'Yes, at first.'

'You don't sound very happy. Did she take to it better than you expected?'

Alessandra thought for a moment. 'She appeared to, but I think that's only because she wanted to please Fabrizio.'

'Did she keep climaxing? If she did then she must have been enjoying it. She couldn't have managed that just to please Fabrizio.'

'She had several orgasms.'

'I do wish I'd been there,' said Leonora regretfully. 'I think it was mean of Fabrizio not to let us all watch.'

'She'd have panicked and run away. She was horrified when she realised I was in the room.'

'Tell me exactly what happened,' begged Leonora.

Alessandra gave a small sigh. 'I'm too tired. Anyway, it wasn't that interesting.'

'But it must have been! Why isn't she down to breakfast?'

'I expect she's ashamed of herself. She probably can't believe the things she allowed us to do to her.'

Leonora smiled. 'How delicious. Well, I'll simply have to wait until I'm allowed to join in. When's her next session scheduled for?'

Alessandra got to her feet. 'You'll have to ask your brother. I'm going to ring my agent. He said I might need to fly to Milan tomorrow for a shoot.'

'I wouldn't leave now if I were you,' Leonora cautioned her. 'If Megan takes to the life too well you need to be around. You know how fickle my brother is.'

'I don't need you to remind me,' retorted Alessandra.

'I was only trying to be helpful. There's no need to snap my head off.'

Alessandra gave a half smile. 'I'm sorry, I really am. Watching her last night was harder than I'd expected. I enjoyed it when she begged for mercy, but not when she was pleasured. I didn't expect her to like it at all. I suppose I half hoped she'd panic and run out of the room. This game isn't my idea of fun, but I have to play it because of Fabrizio.'

'I wouldn't do anything I didn't want to do just for a man,' said Leonora.

'It's different for you, you're not obsessed with Renato. Sex is what matters to you. It used to be like that for me, until I met your brother.'

'Don't take everything so seriously,' said Leonora. 'Fabrizio will hate it if you start getting moody. He sees this as a piece of fun, a game, nothing more. Games do have endings you know.'

'The trouble is, I don't know what the ending of this one's going to be, do I?'

'Yes you do. Megan's six-month contract will run out, by which time Fabrizio will have tired of her and she'll return to the wilds of Lincolnshire a sexually wiser young woman.'

'I suppose so,' agreed Alessandra. 'Now, I'm going to ring my agent.'

Alone in the room Leonora wondered what to do for the morning. She knew that her brother wanted Renato to go over some figures with him, which meant that if she wanted to ride she'd have to ride alone. Not that she minded; it made no difference to her whether she had a companion or not. The main difference was that when Renato was with her they'd stop after a while and make love in a field or wood before returning to the house. She supposed that today she'd have to be content to wait for Renato to be free that evening. Or better still, perhaps the pair of them would be allowed to take part in the next stage of Megan's initiation.

She took her favourite chestnut gelding, the one Megan had seen her with, and rode him hard over the Sussex Downs for an hour before returning to the house. There was no sign of a stable boy which meant that she had to lead the horse back to his stall herself. After taking off his saddle and rubbing him down she made sure he had plenty of food and water then turned to leave the stable. To her surprise a figure was blocking the entrance.

'Franco! What are you doing here?'

'I wanted to see you.'

'Fine, now you've seen me. Get out of my way, I want to go into the house.' Franco didn't move. 'Did you hear me?' asked Leonora dangerously. 'I said, get out of my way.'

'Perhaps I don't want to.'

'I shan't ask you a third time,' she said quietly.

Franco's blue eyes were ice cold. 'I didn't imagine that you would.'

Leonora looked at him for a moment, tapping the handle of her riding crop against a thigh-length boot. Suddenly, without any warning, she raised her whip and slashed at Franco's upper arm. He didn't even wince with pain and before she had a moment to realise what was happening he'd raised his other arm and struck her a stinging blow across her left cheek. Taken by surprise she stumbled backwards and almost fell.

'How dare you!' she cried.

'You hit me first,' he pointed out.

'If I tell Fabrizio about this ...'

'But you won't, will you?' asked Franco, advancing steadily on Leonora and forcing her to retreat until her back was up against the wall of the stable. 'You won't tell him because you're enjoying yourself.'

Reaching out, his left hand caught hold of her right breast while his right hand forced its way roughly between her thighs, his fingers grabbing her crotch, squeezing her tightly until she squealed.

'This is how you like it, isn't it? Quick and rough?'

Leonora wriggled, trying desperately to free herself from his grip. 'I don't want you touching me,' she hissed. 'I'm warning you, let go of me or there'll be serious trouble.'

He smiled thinly. 'I'm not afraid of you, Leonora. I understand you very well.' All the time he was talking his hand was tightening around her breast and his palm was moving roughly against the fabric of the jodhpurs between her thighs. Her breathing grew more rapid and although she continued to struggle, she knew that she was becoming aroused.

He moved quickly, his hands now grabbing her wrists and pinioning them against the wall as he pressed his body against hers. She could feel his erection through his trousers as it pressed against her belly; the more she struggled the harder his erection grew.

The air in the stable was warm and the gelding shifted restlessly in its stall, disturbed by what was happening. Franco bent his head and covered Leonora's mouth with his, his tongue forcing its way past her teeth, moving in and out as though she was giving him head. She continued to struggle, but less convincingly, and she could feel the blood racing through her veins as desire flared in her.

'You want me don't you?' he said triumphantly.

'No,' she said coldly, determined that he shouldn't know how much he was turning her on.

'What a little liar you are,' he said contemptuously.

'Let go of me,' cried Leonora, and for a brief moment she managed to free one of her hands. She struck out at him, catching him a glancing blow on the chest that scarcely registered on his muscular torso.

'Is that the best you can do?' he asked. 'I can do much better than that.' With brutal savagery he tore open her riding shirt, and as she gasped at the feeling of the stable air on her naked breasts he slapped each of her nipples in turn, then pinched the rapidly reddening tips until she was writhing in an ecstasy of pain and excitement. She was so damp that her juices had already soaked through her panties and into her jodh-purs. Now Franco's hand returned between her thighs and he laughed at the evidence of her arousal.

'You see, I wasn't wrong. Tell me that you want me. Tell me that you want to feel me inside you. That's all you have to do and I'll take you here and now.'

Leonora was furious at the way her body was betraying her. This wasn't the way she liked her sex at all, and she couldn't understand why she was so turned on. She *did* want him to take her, to plunge himself into her and fill the hungry, demanding space that was crying out for satisfaction, but she knew that she'd never forgive herself if she allowed it to happen.

Thinking rapidly, she abruptly allowed her body to go limp and for a moment Franco relaxed his grip. The instant he did, Leonora kicked out at him catching him an agonising blow in the testicles so that he fell away from her, doubled up and groaning. 'Go on then,' she taunted him. Take me now.'

'You bitch!' he snarled. 'You've made sure that I can't.'

'Call yourself a man,' she jeered, exhilaration filling her now that she'd turned the tables on him.

'I'm more of a man than Renato,' he gasped, trying to regain control of his breathing. 'I've always known it and now you do too. When you tire of him, let me know. I don't intend to give you any more demonstrations of what we'd be like together.'

'I'm very glad to hear it,' snapped Leonora, and as she walked past him to leave the stable she struck him a final blow on his back with her riding whip. He yelped in pain but his eyes were filled with lust and Leonora's belly quivered for a moment at the thought of what sex with him would be like.

Back in the house she hurried up to the room she shared with Renato, ran herself a hot bath and threw all her clothes into the linen basket. She didn't want to think about what had happened, or how close she'd come to letting Franco take her. She knew that he wouldn't ever force her to be subservient, but sex between them would always be a fight, their passion fuelled by a strange love-hate relationship in which her desire to dominate might not always triumph. She wasn't certain that she could live with that.

After her bath she lay face down on the bed and masturbated to release the tension that had built up during their encounter. Normally she was able to delay gratification for as long as she liked, but not today. Today the sharp, all-consuming contractions came quickly and her body shuddered violently as her fingers plunged in and out of her vagina while her thumb toyed with her clitoris.

Afterwards, as she lay stretched languorously on the bed, her breathing gradually slowing, she wondered again how Megan was feeling this morning.

Megan sat at the desk in the library looking through the notes of her meeting with the antique book dealer of the previous evening, but it was difficult for her to concentrate. Her mind was still full of all that had happened to her the night before, and she was finding it impossible to believe that she'd allowed Fabrizio and his lover to treat her as they had. The easiest thing to do was to blame Fabrizio for teaching her to need pleasure, but she knew that she couldn't totally hold him responsible. The things they'd done to her last night had opened her eyes to an entirely different kind of sexuality, a sexuality that she was forced to admit to herself she'd enjoyed. Certainly she'd been afraid, and at times there'd been pain, but that had only served to deepen the pleasure and increase the depth of her response. She could hardly blame Fabrizio for that.

She wondered what was going to happen next, whether he was going to suggest that they repeat last night's events, or if that had been his way of telling her that the affair was over. Perhaps, by including Alessandra, he was demonstrating to Megan where his true affections lay. If that was the case she knew that she wouldn't be able to stay here, because although what had happened shamed her, the memory of it was sufficient to re-awaken her need for further excitement. Her body had never felt so alive and responsive.

Pushing away her handwritten notes, she started to put some of the books on the shelves. Sometimes she wondered if this job would ever be finished. There was so much to do, and at the moment so many distractions. If she hadn't become sexually involved with Fabrizio she would be getting more work done. Realising this she understood that he must have planned her seduction from the moment they met, and she wondered why he'd chosen her. No one before him had ever seemed that anxious to seduce her, not even Nick. Clearly the Italian had sensed hidden depths in her, depths that she herself hadn't realised existed.

'How are you getting on?' asked Fabrizio, walking into the library.

Balanced on the top of a stepladder, Megan wobbled precariously and he quickly crossed the floor to steady her. 'Sorry, did I make you jump?'

'I was miles away.'

'What were you thinking about, I wonder?'

She felt confused and embarrassed. 'Last night,' she whispered.

'Oh, you mean your meeting with that man. What was his name?'

'Francis Blakeney, but that wasn't . . . '

'Yes, Francis Blakeney. I believe my uncle mentioned him once or twice in his letters to me. Did Mr Blakeney say that he'd ever met my uncle?'

Megan couldn't understand why Fabrizio was talking about her meeting. Surely he didn't really believe that she'd been thinking about that? He must have known that her mind was on the other things that had happened to her last night; the dark, secret things that had taken place in the second bedroom of the top floor. 'As a matter of fact he did think he remembered him,' she replied curtly.

Fabrizio looked surprised by her tone. 'Are you all right?'

'I suppose so.'

He studied her carefully. 'You're very heavy-eyed. Did you sleep all right?'

'After I left you, do you mean?' she demanded, determined to force him to talk about what had happened.

'Yes, after you'd left Alessandra and I.' He emphasised his lover's name slightly and Megan flinched inwardly. She didn't particularly want to remember Alessandra. It was Fabrizio and what he'd done that dominated her mind.

'I slept very heavily. For the first time I even slept through my alarm this morning,' she said.

'I see. No doubt you were exhausted. How are you getting on here?' He glanced around the room.

Megan felt like screaming at him. She needed to know where she stood, to understand what was happening to her, and she hated the way Fabrizio was toying with her. 'I've never done anything like last night before,' she said quietly as she descended the stepladder to the floor. 'I feel confused.'

'In what way confused?'

'I don't know what happens next.'

Fabrizio opened a book on Italian sculpture and flicked through the photographs. 'Ah, look, here's a picture of Sansovino's *Bacchus and a Faun*. The original was life-size and he used to make an assistant of his called Pippo del Sabbro stand naked, posing for most of every day. They say that posing naked in the cold drove the poor man mad and he died a few years later. Apparently, before his death he used to walk around wrapped in a cloth as if he were a clay model, and strike attitudes as a prophet or a soldier. I expect the story's an exaggeration, but there's always a price to be paid for anything truly wonderful, don't you think?'

'I've never thought about it,' confessed Megan. 'I suppose you're right but in this case I don't see what the assistant got out of it. He didn't have the satisfaction of creating anything.'

'But he helped to create something,' said Fabrizio. 'To be a partner, an accomplice, that too is wonderful, as you discovered last night.' Megan felt her face redden. 'I've embarrassed you, I'm sorry. That was not the intention. It was wonderful to see you entering so whole-heartedly into the pleasures of the flesh. I have a replica of this statue in my office. I will show it to you sometime. It is truly magnificent.'

'You still haven't answered my question,' persisted Megan.

'What question?'

'I want to know what happens next?'

Fabrizio smiled. 'That rather depends on you. I take it you're still eager to enjoy the pleasures that I have taught you?'

Megan lowered her head, wishing that she didn't have to reply. 'Yes,' she muttered.

'Excellent. Meet me in the games room on the second floor at nine o'clock tonight. If you remember, I showed it to you when you came for your interview.'

'The games room?'

'Yes. Sometimes we enjoy an evening of game playing.'

'That wasn't exactly what I had in mind,' said Megan.

'You may enjoy it more than you expect,' said Fabrizio. 'It will be interesting to see.'

'I don't know many card games,' confessed Megan, 'and I hate charades or anything like that.'

Fabrizio caught hold of her shoulders and immediately she was swamped with desire for him. 'This won't be a charade, Megan. The games that we play are not the games that other people play. I would have expected you to credit me with more imagination than that.'

Her breathing quickened. 'How many people take part in these games?'

'It varies, but tonight it will simply be myself and Alessandra, Leonora and Renato.'

'And me?'

Fabrizio nodded. 'Yes, you. You are very important to my enjoyment of the evening, *cara*. I hope you understand that?'

She'd been hesitating, afraid of what might lie ahead

of her, but his words were encouraging. She was able to believe that she was important to him, and she needed to be important to him almost as much as she needed the pleasure that he gave her. 'What if I don't like one of the games?'

'You will enjoy all the games,' he said firmly. 'Trust me. Having seen you last night I know that I was not mistaken about you. As I had hoped, you are fitting perfectly into our little household, and things will only get better. But remember what I've said. Sometimes, like the sculptor's assistant of long ago, it is necessary to suffer a little if the final goal is to be reached.'

Megan's mouth felt dry. 'And what is the final goal?'

'When you get there you will know,' he said quietly.

Although Megan worked hard for the rest of the day, even giving up her lunch hour because she was falling behind, she couldn't forget his words or stop wondering about what would happen to her later that night.

Chapter Seven

Pausing outside the door to the games room, Megan
listened. She could hear voices inside, a low constant
murmuring sound, and then, just as she was about to
enter, she heard an unmistakable cry of ecstasy. Her
body began to shake and the palms of her hands grew
damp. She wondered whether she should go back to
the safety of her own room, but curiosity and sexual
need drove her on.

As she'd come to expect from Fabrizio, the room
was in darkness. Only two large spotlights were con-
centrated at the far end, where Alessandra was sitting
on a raised platform, her back supported by a pile of
cushions and her wrists and ankles cuffed. The cuffs

looked to be made of leather and the two wrist chains joined together to form one long chain, then divided into two again between Alessandra's thighs. This meant that she could be adjusted to almost any position other people desired. It also meant that she was entirely helpless.

Despite the fact that Megan crept as quietly as possible into the room, Renato heard her arrive. He walked over to her. 'You're just in time to take part. Alessandra's well away now.'

'What do you mean?'

'We're all taking it in turns to pleasure her. The first one of us to fail has to drop out and so on, until eventually we get a winner.'

Megan was stunned. 'Is this the kind of game you usually play?'

'Not always. Sometimes we really do play cards.' She could hear the laughter in his voice, but it was kind laughter and she didn't mind. What she did mind was the fact that she was expected to become a participant in what was happening.

'Ah, you've timed your arrival to perfection,' said Fabrizio, stepping down from the platform as Alessandra's body continued to shake from the orgasm he'd just given her. 'I think she needs a woman's touch now. Let's see what you can do with her.'

Megan stared at him, wishing that she could make out his expression in the darkness.

'What's the matter?' he continued. 'Don't you like giving other people pleasure?'

'I've never touched another woman before,' she admitted.

'Then now's a good time to start. Alessandra enjoys the feminine touch. Not always Leonora's I have to say; she can be a little rough. I imagine you'll be more to her taste.'

'I can't,' protested Megan.

'Indeed? Then you'll have to leave. You can't stay here if you're not going to play.'

'Will you come to me later if I leave?' she whispered, ashamed to ask but needing to find out.

'Certainly not. I want you to learn to enjoy the things that I enjoy, and I'm enjoying this.'

'If she won't do it, I will,' said Leonora, walking purposefully towards the platform. 'It isn't fair to leave Alessandra too long between climaxes. She'll lose her rhythm.'

'Stay where you are,' commanded Fabrizio. 'It's Megan's turn.'

Renato put a comforting hand between Megan's shoulders. 'Alessandra likes you. It won't be difficult to give her pleasure.'

Trapped in the two spotlights Alessandra's eyes stared out into the gloom and Megan could see that the beautiful model was waiting for her. Slowly, astonished at her own actions, Megan began to walk towards her. She half stumbled up the two wooden blocks to the platform and then looked down at the other girl.

Alessandra was wearing nothing except for a half cup black lace bra, which thrust her breasts upwards so that the tiny delicate pink nipples were visible. Hesitantly, Megan reached down and touched one of the puckered buds, and she heard Alessandra's quick intake of breath. Emboldened by this she began to stroke the nipple between finger and thumb until it grew harder.

'Excellent,' called Fabrizio from the back of the room.

'Am I allowed to give her any instructions?' asked Alessandra.

Leonora moved towards the platform. 'No. That would be cheating.'

'But she isn't doing it right,' complained Alessandra.

'Give her time,' said Renato.

Megan knelt on the floor so that she was on a level with Alessandra. Remembering how much she'd liked the feel of Fabrizio's breath on her own breasts, she bent her head and blew lightly through the lace bra, while at the same time massaging the imprisoned nipple between her finger and thumb. Alessandra's eyelids drooped and she gave a languorous sigh. For the first time ever Megan felt a surge of sexual power over another person and was surprised at how much pleasure she took from it.

For several minutes she toyed with Alessandra's breasts and then she started to massage the exposed, naked belly of the chained girl. Initially her touch was tentative but then, as her excitement grew and she felt her own nipples stiffening, it became firmer. Soon Alessandra's hips were writhing. Now Megan allowed her hand to stray between Alessandra's thighs. The girl was very damp and Megan saw that her sex lips were pink and swollen, fully opened to expose the glistening flesh within.

As the tip of Megan's finger touched the damp flesh, Alessandra's hips jerked and Megan's belly tightened in response. She could feel the sexual tension rising in herself and, casting aside her inhibitions, she circled her finger round and round the centre of Alessandra's pleasure, working to a steady rhythm as Alessandra began to utter tiny guttural groans. 'Yes, oh yes!' cried the Italian girl.

Megan could see that Alessandra was close to coming and she wanted to feel the other girl's climax, so she thrust two fingers deep inside her while at the same time continuing to massage the ever-hardening bud with her thumb.

With a sharp cry Alessandra came. Megan was astonished at how strong the model's internal muscles were as they tightened powerfully around her fingers, seeming to suck at them, drawing them deeper inside her as the strong contractions of the orgasm pulsated through her imprisoned body.

Megan was delighted at her success. She didn't want to stop; she wanted to carry on giving this beautiful creature pleasure because it was giving her pleasure too. There was an ache between her own thighs and tiny tingles were darting through her lower belly.

'It's Renato's turn now,' called Leonora. 'You'll get another go soon enough.'

Suddenly ashamed of herself, Megan hurried away

from Alessandra and into the welcoming darkness of the room.

'You did well,' murmured Fabrizio. 'Did it turn you on?' Without waiting for an answer he slid a hand inside the opening of Megan's blouse and felt her breast and the rigid tip of her nipple. 'Clearly it did. Good, that's what it's meant to do.'

Megan couldn't see what Renato was doing to Alessandra as his body was shielding the other girl from her, but she could hear tiny cries of protest as he moved her around. It seemed that his ways were not as much to Alessandra's liking as Megan's had been, because all at once there was a loud 'No!' from Alessandra, followed by a cry of pain which made Megan's heart leap.

'Her pleasure will come,' Fabrizio assured Megan. 'How would you like to take her place in a minute?'

'Take her place?' asked Megan in horror.

'That's right. Even Alessandra can't go on for ever and so far no one's had to drop out.'

'You can't ask that of me,' whispered Megan.

'I can ask anything of you,' he said softly. 'What I can't do is make you say yes.'

Megan turned her head towards the platform, and as

she did so Alessandra uttered a scream that was a mixture of pain and pleasure, a sound like no other that Megan had ever heard. Although it frightened her it also excited her, and she wanted to know what it was like to experience a sensation as intense as that.

'All right,' she said abruptly.

She sensed that Fabrizio was taken aback. 'You're willing to take her place now?'

'That's what you want isn't it?'

'Yes.'

'Then I will. I don't want to spoil your game.'

She felt his fingers caress her jawline, and his lips brushed lightly against each of her eyelids in turn. 'How right I was about you,' he murmured and then raised his voice. 'If you've finished, Renato, then release Alessandra. Megan's going to take her place. The trouble with you Alessandra is that you come too easily. Megan will make the game more difficult for the rest of us.'

'Do we have to start from the beginning again?' asked Leonora querulously.

Her brother seemed puzzled by the question. 'What do you mean?'

'I mean we were just working up to the more

sophisticated things with Alessandra. Do we have to go back to basics with Megan?'

'Not at all. You can do what you like with her. I believe you have first go Leonora.'

'Shouldn't I have first go?' asked Alessandra as, freed from her bonds, she began to dress herself.

'No, you need time to catch your breath. I want Leonora to start but first I have to get the cuffs on Megan. Come,' he continued, catching hold of Megan's wrist, 'I will make you as comfortable as possible. However, do not worry if you fail to climax. It is time that someone dropped out.'

Megan found it difficult to imagine that she'd be able to come at all. She was beginning to wonder why on earth she'd agreed to this. Her legs felt as though they'd turned to jelly, and as Fabrizio led her up onto the platform and then began to undress her, she looked down at the floor, unable to face everyone in the room.

Fabrizio's fingers flicked beneath her chin. 'Head up, shoulders back, you must display yourself as well as possible.'

Megan felt anxious. 'Do the cuffs hurt?'

'Of course not. They're simply a form of restraint, so

that we can turn you in any way we like. It adds to the excitement for us all, you included.'

'What if I don't like what someone does to me?'

'Once the cuffs are on they don't come off until the game is ended. It's up to you. Do you want them on or not?' He waited, holding the two sets of leather cuffs in his hands.

Megan tried to put her fear to one side. She'd come this far, it would be stupid to turn back now. 'All right,' she agreed.

Swiftly, Fabrizio fastened them so that there was plenty of slack for both her wrists and her ankles. 'If anyone wants to tighten them they can but it's usually easier to give you a reasonable amount of freedom.' As he spoke he eased her back against the cushions, then he pushed her thighs apart, bending her knees outwards but pulling her feet together. After studying her for a few minutes he placed a cushion beneath her buttocks and she realised that her entire vulva was totally exposed. 'That looks perfect,' he said with satisfaction. 'Let the game continue.'

Leonora was quickly on to the platform, and looking up into her eyes Megan felt a frisson of fear. There was something about the way the Italian girl was looking at her, the obvious delight she was taking from Megan's position of bondage, that was chilling. 'Am I allowed to do whatever I like?' Leonora called out.

'No,' replied Fabrizio.

'But you said we can carry on from where we were with Alessandra.'

'You can be experimental, but not extreme.'

'Did you hear that?' asked Leonora, looking down at the tethered Megan. 'How does it make you feel?'

Megan didn't know what to say. Her mouth had gone dry and she was shaking, yet she was excited too. 'I'm not sure what he means,' she confessed.

'How sweet,' said Leonora, who didn't sound as though she thought it sweet at all. 'I'll have to show you then.' She walked away into the shadows of the room for a moment, and when she returned she was carrying a small canvas bag.

Within minutes she was pouring scented oil from a bottle into her left hand, and then she began to slowly massage it over Megan's lower belly, pressing firmly against the tingling flesh, her fingers moving between the folds of Megan's thighs. They moved back and forth in an insidiously arousing caress that made Megan's whole pubic area ache. She squirmed restlessly but Leonora flicked her breasts hard with her fingers, causing Megan to squeal. 'You're not meant to help me bring you to orgasm. If anything you're meant to try and defeat me. Don't you understand anything about the game?'

'I'm sorry,' said Megan. But her body was now so frantic for satisfaction that she was terrified of Leonora stopping.

'I like an apology,' said Leonora with a smile. At last her fingers brushed softly over the crisp curls of Megan's pubic hair and Megan felt herself opening beneath the other girl's expert touch.

The oiled fingers moved lower, sliding over Megan's damp flesh. 'She's very wet,' said Leonora loudly. 'It seems you're not as shy as I'd expected,' she added, glancing at Megan. 'I don't think I need to wait any longer.' With that she reached into her bag once more and Megan gasped as she saw what Leonora took out.

It was a vibrator, at least four inches long and two inches wide. At the top was a thick bulbous head. Megan's hips pressed back against the cushions. The vibrator looked large and threatening.

'Don't start being difficult,' said Leonora. 'This is what you need. Don't you ache inside? Isn't your little clit throbbing? Come on, tell me the truth.' She was right, but Megan wasn't going to admit it. Once more her thighs were pressed apart, so wide that her muscles ached. This meant that she was now fully opened and she watched with increasing tension as Leonora covered the large end of the vibrator with some of the oil before moving it against Megan's entrance.

Megan's muscles tightened. She was afraid of this invasion, but Leonora quickly played with Megan's clitoris again, drawing small spirals around the base of the stem and allowing her oiled fingers to skim over the unbelievably sensitive tip until Megan's breath snagged in her throat and her breathing became harsh and ragged.

The ache between her thighs was unbearable now and she heard herself begin to moan. This was the signal for Leonora to start inserting the vibrator. As the head stretched the opening to Megan's vagina she whimpered with discomfort, but with one swift, skilled movement Leonora twisted and pushed until it was inside the hot throbbing flesh. At last Megan's ache eased and a deliciously satisfying full sensation spread through her.

Leonora proceeded to use her free hand to massage

Megan's throbbing breasts, moving from one to the other and occasionally bending her head and drawing her tongue across the surface of both. At the same time the vibrator began to move inside Megan, sending pulsating sensations through her, and she felt the hot tightness of an impending orgasm. The head of the vibrator was touching the tip of her cervix – she'd never been so full – and all at once she couldn't contain the mounting pressure any longer and a huge wave of ecstatic pleasure crashed over her, like water escaping from a dam.

Her body jerked and spasmed, and she cried out in a frenzy of delight, yet still the vibrator continued to stimulate her nerve endings so that the orgasm went on and on until the muscular contractions became painful. The pleasure remained, but it was a darker pleasure, and one which, if she was honest with herself, Megan found even more fulfilling.

'She's coming, in case you hadn't noticed,' called Renato. 'That's the end of your turn, Leonora.'

'You enjoyed that didn't you?' Leonora whispered.

Megan looked up at her, her eyes huge and filled with a mixture of pleasure and disbelief. 'It was incredible.'

'Believe me, I can give you more pleasure than that, and I will as the days go by,' promised the other girl. Bending down she gave Megan's left nipple a sharp tweak and then moved away. A flash of pain shot through Megan's breast but she shivered with delight, a delight that was quickly followed by shame at what she was allowing to happen.

Renato swiftly took his place on the platform and within five minutes he'd brought Megan to another climax, using only his hands and mouth on her. His touch was so skilful, so unerring that her heightened senses were easily inflamed. As she writhed beneath his touch, almost sobbing with ecstasy, he spoke.

'Be very careful, Megan. These people are dangerous.'

She heard the words, but they meant nothing to her. All that mattered at this moment was pleasure, the pleasure that they were giving her, and she couldn't understand what he was warning her about.

Alessandra was next. She too tried to bring Megan to a climax using her fingers and mouth, but Megan's body was tired and no matter what Alessandra did she was unable to climax. When Alessandra sucked on Megan's nipples, and nipped at the brown areolae with her teeth, her fingers moving in and out of Megan's soaking pussy, Megan felt certain that she was going to come. All the tension was there, even the heavy pulse behind her clitoris, but just when she expected sweet release her body betrayed her and the sensations started to die away. She moaned in frustration.

It had been so easy until then, but now, stranded at the point of no return and unable to come she became horribly aware of the fact that she was being watched. This had the effect of making her climax recede further. Then, as she began to think about what she must look like and recalled Renato's words the sexual tension dissipated entirely and she realised that she wasn't going to climax.

'What's the matter?' asked Alessandra urgently. 'Don't let me down or I shall have to drop out.'

'You're not allowed to talk to her,' called Fabrizio. 'It's your fault Alessandra, you didn't use enough initiative. You're out I'm afraid. Now I believe it's my turn.'

As Fabrizio stood over Megan she glanced up at him. He looked even taller than usual, as though he was looming over her, a dark frightening presence which threatened and yet at the same time aroused her. 'It seems you're harder to please than Alessandra,' he said. 'Since I have no intention of being knocked out of the game at this stage, I must make certain that I succeed where she failed.'

'I didn't mean Alessandra to fail,' said Megan. 'I tried but ...'

'You're not meant to speak unless it's in response to a question,' Fabrizio reminded her. 'You see this?'

Looking up, Megan saw that in his right hand he held a strange-looking implement. The base clearly identified it as a vibrator but the long, thin stem was covered in graduated beads, and when Fabrizio ran his hand over them she saw that the stem was flexible.

'What is it?' she asked nervously.

'How many times do I have to remind you not to speak?' He was becoming annoyed and Megan bit on her bottom lip, afraid to apologise but anxious to appease him. She was horrified at how rapidly she was learning to subjugate her instinctive reactions to his instructions. This wasn't at all the kind of girl she'd thought herself to be, but since she wanted the pleasure that Fabrizio could give her she was willing to do almost anything in order to obtain it.

'I'll answer your question,' he continued. 'As you can see this is a sophisticated vibrator, but I intend to use it differently from the way you may imagine. I hope you find the experience as exciting as I will.'

Megan watched him kneel beside her, and then he was turning her over onto her stomach, pushing the pillows beneath her belly and breasts and she looked back over her shoulder. Roughly he tangled his fingers in her hair and turned her head until she was face down again. 'You're not to look. I think we need another cushion beneath your hips,' he added thoughtfully. Now her lower torso was raised higher than her head, creating a pressure on her lower belly and at the same time leaving her buttocks exposed to the gaze of the spectators in the room.

She felt both humiliated and afraid and when Fabrizio's lips touched the nape of her neck she jumped in alarm. He murmured something in Italian, she had no idea what, and proceeded to let his tongue lick gently down her spine until the tension eased out of her. When he came to the cleft between her buttocks he pressed his lips firmly down on the flesh, kissing and sucking at the spot until she started to move her hips. By doing this she was able to generate pressure on her pubic bone, and indirectly her clitoris, so that at last the first flickers of rising pleasure darted through her.

'That's better,' he whispered, and now his hands were cupping her rounded buttocks, his fingers moving over the flesh and down into the creases beneath. She felt him spread her legs apart, as wide apart as was possible with the cuffs on her ankles. She wondered what everyone could see, whether they knew, as she did, that her pubic hair was slick with moisture as she grew more and more excited. Now Fabrizio slid a hand under her breasts, tickling teasingly around the nipples until they hardened. He gave a small sigh of contentment. When he withdrew his hand she wanted to protest, but knew that there was no point. This had to be done his way.

His hands returned to her buttocks and he massaged some oil into them, allowing it to trickle from the base of her spine between the two carefully separated globes so that it seeped onto her vulva. She felt her sex lips begin to swell and lifted her hips a little because she wanted to feel the oil moving against her clitoris, but it was impossible.

His hands were moving rapidly now, still massaging her buttocks but also sliding beneath her, pressing against her entire vulva, and a delicious hot tingling sensation started to spread between her thighs. She was totally relaxed, but at the same time tension was mounting within her and she knew that her body was moving towards a climax, a climax which wasn't imminent but which she was confident would come as long as he continued to touch her in these wonderful ways.

Then, with cruel abruptness, his hand left her vulva and he began doing something that no one had ever done to her before, something that caused her body to tense in protest. He started to ease a lubricated finger into the puckered opening between the rounded cheeks of her bottom. She tried to roll away from him but he was too quick for her, sitting on the top of her thighs so that she was unable to move. 'Be still,' he commanded her. 'Soon you will know exquisite pleasure.'

As the tip of his finger intruded into the secret opening, she panicked. 'Please stop,' she cried, 'I don't like it.'

'Haven't you learnt to trust me yet?' he asked. His finger was now inside the tight little opening, moving around and pressing very softly against the inside walls.

Megan felt her bowels cramp, and her first instinct was to bear down and expel his finger. 'Breathe through your mouth,' he instructed her.

Because she wanted to please him, and because some strangely exciting sensations were already filling her lower body, she did as he said. Immediately the cramping stopped and now her hips were writhing for a different reason. A deep, sweet aching pleasure was spreading from between her buttocks to behind her pubic bone, and it felt as though her insides were turning to liquid. 'That's better,' she heard him murmur as he withdrew his finger.

Megan relaxed. Her clitoris was hard, her breasts full, and she knew that if he pressed against her vulva she would come easily. He'd been right, it hadn't been bad at all, and she'd liked the sensation. She was so carried away with relief that she completely forgot what he'd been holding in his hand earlier until she felt the cool, smooth roundness of a tiny bead pressing where his finger had been only seconds earlier.

'No!' she wailed, but Fabrizio ignored her. Very gradually, with deliberately cruel slowness, he inserted the flexible bead-covered wand inside her second opening until she felt so full that the pleasurable ache deepened to a dull throbbing pressure that was closer to pain.

'Keep breathing through your mouth,' he reminded her and then he switched on the vibrator. The sensations produced by the beads rolling against the paper-thin walls of her rectum, were amazing. It was as though somebody was sending electric currents through her body, and at times the current was too strong, so that she whimpered as her screaming nerve endings were overloaded. Then, every time she thought that she could take no more, the pain would turn into a heavy liquid pleasure that made her belly swell.

Megan could feel her legs thrashing helplessly, restrained by the ankle cuffs, and her whole body was shuddering as the tension mounted inexorably inside her. Fabrizio put his free hand beneath her, his fingers digging deep into the soft flesh of her belly, and again she uttered a muttered cry of protest because the skin felt stretched to breaking point, the muscles rippling and spasming in shock as the vibrator continued its remorseless massage.

'You're nearly there,' he told her. 'I can tell. I think I'll increase the speed.'

'No, don't!' cried Megan. 'I can't bear any more.'

But he ignored her and as the beads vibrated harder against the already frantic soft inner tissue her orgasm finally crashed over her and she screamed with a mixture of pain and bitter-sweet release. The contractions seemed to go on and on, and only when the last ripples died away did Fabrizio turn off the strange wand. As he removed it she felt every bead popping out of her, and her flesh jumped because she felt so tender that that sensation was more than she wanted.

'Next time it will be me inside you there, not the wand,' he said, his mouth touching the skin behind her ear. 'I want to feel you beneath me, writhing as you were writhing then, while I spill myself into you.'

Megan shuddered, not from fear but from a terrible depraved excitement, an excitement that shamed her but which she couldn't suppress. She remained face down on the pillows, her body limp and exhausted, her skin covered with droplets of sweat and waited to see what was going to happen next.

In fact, Fabrizio had made sure that he won the game. Leonora and Renato tried to bring Megan's exhausted, sated body to further peaks of pleasure, but both of them failed. 'You'll get better at this,' Leonora promised, when she had to leave the platform defeated.

'Soon even the sight of my riding crop will be enough to bring you to the edge of an orgasm. You're learning fast, but as yet you're still a novice in this house. I'm longing for the day when you allow your sexuality to blossom fully.'

Megan didn't reply; she didn't have the energy. Also, she simply didn't believe that she was capable of more than this. Feeling as though she were in a strange dream she watched as Fabrizio unfastened her and then she was putting on her clothes while the drapes were drawn back and the outside world was allowed to intrude once more.

'We're going to have a drink before we go to bed,' said Fabrizio casually. 'Do you want to join us?'

Megan opened her mouth to say yes. Then, when she remembered what she must have looked like, tethered and naked on the platform, and remembered too what the others had done to her, she lost her courage. They were all behaving as though nothing out of the ordinary had happened, yet it had and she couldn't forget that. 'I think I'll go to bed,' she replied.

Fabrizio looked hard at her. 'As you wish,' he said pleasantly. 'I hope you sleep well.' As she walked past him he caught hold of her arm. 'Tomorrow, Alessandra flies to Milan for a fashion shoot,' he whispered. You can spend the night with me, just the two of us. We should have an exciting time.'

Megan was thrilled. This was what she really wanted, to have Fabrizio to herself, making love to her as he had done in the beginning, before he started playing these strange games with her. 'That'll be wonderful,' she muttered, worried in case Alessandra should overhear.

As the door closed behind Megan, Alessandra glanced at her lover. 'I suppose you told her I'm going to Milan?' He nodded. 'Remember your advice to the rest of us,' Alessandra cautioned him. 'You nearly went too far tonight. Alone with her, there will be no one to reign you in.'

'You seem to have very little faith in my judgement,' said Fabrizio. 'I assure you, things are going so well that the last thing I would do is spoil them. She believes that there can be nothing more decadent than tonight. It will be interesting to see how she reacts when she realises what a long way she has to go before she truly fits in with this household.'

'She seems a natural submissive,' said Leonora. 'It's a pity she doesn't react better to other women.'

'She will,' said Renato. 'At the moment she's fixated on Fabrizio, but as she becomes more addicted to the pleasures of the flesh rather than an emotional attachment she'll give herself over to anyone who can supply the extra stimulation she needs. The time will come when she has to move on, and that's when you'll come into your own with her.'

Leonora smiled. 'Let's hope it doesn't take too long.'

Chapter Eight

The following morning Leonora wandered in a desultory fashion around the house. Alessandra had left for Milan, Renato and Fabrizio were shut away in Fabrizio's study and, as usual, Megan was working in the library. Leonora was bored. To make matters worse she was frustrated.

Last night, when she and Renato had returned to their room, she'd been eagerly looking forward to a long session with him. At first all had gone well, but when she'd attempted to tie his hands above his head as he lay spreadeagle on the bed beneath her, for the first time that she could remember a look of irritation had crossed his face and he'd moved away. When she'd asked him why he'd claimed that he felt tired, but she knew that wasn't the real reason.

She'd watched him very carefully earlier in the evening, when Megan had been the victim on the platform, and had noticed how his eyes had never strayed from the English girl. Obviously he was turned on by her, which wasn't surprising, but Leonora couldn't believe that he found their visitor's submissiveness more attractive than Leonora's taste for domination. Although, when they first met, Renato had been a somewhat reluctant participant in the kind of sex that she enjoyed the most, she thought that he'd become as keen on it as she was. Certainly they'd suited each other well, until now.

Leonora walked into the kitchen. One of the maids was there looking enquiringly at her. 'Can I help you, signorina?'

'Just get out,' snapped Leonora. 'If I want anything I'll make it for myself.'

The maid, who was used to the strange ways of the household, departed without a word. Leonora had once had an exciting sex session with her, but the girl had complained to Fabrizio who'd forbidden Leonora from repeating the experience. She filled the kettle with water and plugged it in, then gazed out of the window over the sink and wondered what on earth she was going to do for the rest of the morning. She'd already been for a ride and although she'd managed to climax several times by gripping the horse firmly with her thighs and rubbing herself against the saddle, she still wasn't satisfied. She needed to feel a man inside her, and along with her frustration a niggling fear was beginning to creep into her mind. What would she do if Renato stopped being the perfect partner for her?

'Where are the staff?' asked Franco, walking into the kitchen.

'Right here,' snapped Leonora, giving him a contemptuous glance.

'Do you mean me?' Franco enquired, and Leonora nodded. 'I see. Perhaps I should have said the domestic staff.'

'Perhaps you should. Maria was in here, but I sent her away. I decided I'm old enough to make my own coffee now.'

'Goodness, how grown up,' he said mockingly. 'Where's Renato?'

'Working with my brother.'

'Of course. I was told to keep the letters that I did this morning until the pair of them had finished. Have you had your ride?'

'I've been out on the horse, if that's what you mean.'

Franco nodded. 'Did he let you down last night?'

'I've no idea what you're talking about. And get out of the way, I want to make my coffee.'

Franco caught hold of her wrist and stopped her halfway across the room. 'Of course you know what I'm talking about. I'm talking about your lover. You've got frustration written all over your beautiful face. Have you had a lovers' quarrel?'

'We never quarrel. Renato's far too reasonable for that.'

'How boring.'

Leonora's top lip curled. 'He isn't in the least boring. Now let go of my wrist.'

'And if I don't?'

'I shall slap you.'

'I wish you would, then I could slap you back. I'm sure you remember what that felt like.'

Leonora was becoming excited. She did remember what it had felt like, and she wanted to experience it again. Swiftly she slapped his face with her free hand. He didn't move for a moment, merely looked at her with his piercing blue eyes, then he imprisoned both her wrists in his right hand and slapped her lightly on each cheek with his left. Her head moved from side to side, her long blonde hair flying out around her head. 'Is that hard enough for you?' he asked.

In reply Leonora lowered her head and bit the hand that was holding her wrist. With a cry of pain Franco released her, but as Leonora moved her leg to knee him he moved swiftly out of the way and pushed her backwards, pinning her shoulders against the wall but being careful to keep her at arm's length.

'You certainly are a little firebrand,' he said admiringly. 'That turns me on, as I'm sure you can see.'

Leonora's eyes moved to his crotch, where there was already an impressive bulge. 'You can be as turned on as you like, only don't expect me to do anything about it.'

'Why not? You want to, you know you do.' His grip on her shoulders eased a little and immediately Leonora flew at him, her fingers going for his face. He jerked his head back and, without knowing quite how it had happened, Leonora found herself clawing frantically at his shirt, tearing at it until the buttons flew onto the floor and she was able to scratch at the tanned flesh beneath.

He winced as one of her long nails drew blood, which she quickly licked away with her tongue, but all the time she continued to scratch at him as an extraordinary charge of sexual energy swept through her. Laughing with delight Franco let her carry on for a few minutes and then, with insulting ease, he turned her around and pushed her towards the kitchen unit, pressing a hand against the back of her shoulders until she found herself with her arms on the unit and her head resting on them.

She felt Franco's hands lifting the skirt of her sundress. Beneath it she was naked except for a tiny G-string which he snapped with one fierce pull of his hand. She was soaking wet now, open and ready, frantic to feel him inside her. At the same time she resented his power over her, the sheer physical strength of him. She began to struggle, kicking out backwards, and she heard him utter a muffled curse. He kept his right hand on the nape of her neck so that her arms and shoulders were pinned to the worktop, while his left hand went around her waist as he pulled her lower body into position. Then he kicked at her feet to adjust her legs.

'This is what you need,' he said thickly, and with no preliminaries at all he thrust himself inside her.

Leonora couldn't restrain a cry of pleasure. Immediately he began to thrust hard, his hips slamming against her buttocks and then, just as she was about to come, he stopped moving. 'Your turn,' he hissed.

Leonora thrust her hips back and forth, desperate to keep her rhythm going, and as she felt the hot, throbbing pulsations begin she tightened her internal muscles around him and heard him groan.

Now they were both moving in a violent rhythm, each concentrating solely on their own pleasure, yet despite this the tempo was perfect for both of them and as Leonora climaxed and her body shuddered with relief she heard Franco gasp and felt his hot seed spilling into her.

Immediately he released her, and by the time she'd straightened up and turned round he'd re-adjusted his clothing and was turning away. She waited for him to tell her how good it had been, how exciting, which was what Renato always did, but he said nothing. Determined not to be the first to speak she switched the kettle back on and began to make her coffee.

'You can make me one while you're about it,' he remarked.

Fury rose in Leonora. Fury at what she'd allowed to happen and fury at the casual way he'd accepted the fact that she'd given herself to him, not during one of their group sexual games but privately, for the sheer pleasure of it. 'I've done enough for you already,' she retorted.

He laughed. 'I didn't realise that was for me. You gave a very good impression of a girl who was enjoying herself.'

'I didn't say I didn't enjoy it, but I knew how much you wanted me and I thought I'd let you have me.'

The look of satisfaction that had previously glittered in his eyes vanished to be replaced by a cold anger that delighted her and at the same time turned her on. 'I'll make you regret saying that,' he snarled.

'I can't wait,' Leonora taunted him. 'What are you going to do? Punish me in front of Fabrizio?'

'Perhaps. Knowing your brother the opportunity's bound to present itself within the structure of a game. Only you and I will know why I make you suffer so much.'

'I'm not afraid of you. I'm not afraid of any man.'

'Perhaps you should be,' he suggested. 'Your position in society, and Renato's adoration make you too self-confident. You need taking in hand.'

'I think I know what I need rather better than you do. How many times do I have to tell you that I like to be in control?'

'You like passion and urgency, that's not necessarily the same thing. You're just afraid that one day you'll find a man who's your equal and you won't be able to cope. You're really a coward.'

'You're the coward,' Leonora retorted. 'You'd never dare surrender control as Renato does.'

'I might, but only if I knew you'd do the same for me. Think about that the next time you're with your lover.'

Alone in the kitchen, Leonora did think about it. She also thought about the way it had felt when he'd taken her so crudely and swiftly. She'd enjoyed it, but she'd also resented him for the way he'd taken control. Now she had to admit to herself that she did find Franco attractive, but she preferred Renato. The question was, did Renato still feel the same about her?

*

Working in the library that afternoon, Megan was joined by Fabrizio. As usual he didn't refer to anything that had happened the previous night, instead he looked around the shelves, examining the books closely.

'I understood that my uncle had an entire collection of Dickens first editions,' he commented. 'Where are they?'

'I'm still putting them together,' explained Megan. 'Why are the books in such a mess? I found Dickens mixed up with Molière. Surely your uncle wasn't that careless. He obviously appreciated good books and I find it hard to believe that he'd have left them in this state.'

'You're quite right. I'm afraid that I made a mistake when we first came over here. I hired someone to sort this out within a week of arriving, but although they claimed to be an expert they were useless. This mess is the result.'

'Then let's hope they didn't walk off with some of the first editions,' said Megan crisply. 'If they did they've walked off with a fortune.'

'Surely it's not the monetary value that matters?' asked Fabrizio. 'As a book-lover, doesn't it concern you more that a collection like that's been split up?'

'Yes, it concerns me, but I'm not certain that's what's happened. They're probably here somewhere. I've got to keep looking, that's all.'

'You're very tenacious, aren't you?'

'I thought that was what you were paying me for.'

'I wasn't only referring to your work.'

'Really?'

He nodded. 'You fascinate me, Megan. Have you telephoned your boyfriend since you arrived here?'

Megan shook her head. 'Nick and I split up just before I came to you. He didn't like the fact that I was giving up a safe job for a short-term one.'

'Have you phoned anyone?'

Megan felt uneasy that this seemed to matter so much to him. 'I've called my friend, Kathy,' she said quickly. 'She encouraged me to reply to your advert.'

'Then we must be very grateful to Kathy. Are you intending to leave us for a weekend to visit her?'

'I have said I might go next weekend,' admitted Megan.

'And now you're having second thoughts?'

'It's simply that I've got a lot to do here,' said Megan, lying through her teeth. She guessed that Fabrizio would know she was lying but she still had to pretend. The truth was that she didn't want to be away from this house, away from the charismatic Italian and his friends who excited her body in so many incredible ways that she couldn't imagine being without them.

'Your dedication to your work does you credit,' he said dryly. 'Don't forget now, tonight you come to my room.'

'Are you sure Alessandra will be away?' asked Megan.

'She's on a modelling assignment. She'll return tomorrow afternoon at the earliest. It will be exciting for us to have time together again, yes?'

'Yes,' agreed Megan fervently, and she spent the rest of the afternoon picturing the way it would be as they lay together in the softness of his bed, Fabrizio the tender, assured lover that he'd shown himself to be when they'd first slept together. Tonight there would be no games, no strange demands made of her, simply an endless night of sensual delight that she could cherish for the rest of her life.

By now Megan was starting to understand Fabrizio, and she realised that it must have been her sexual naïvety which had caught his attention initially. The fact that she was rapidly discovering new things about her sexuality was exciting him, but she knew that she mustn't lose sight of the original reason for the attraction. With that in mind she dressed carefully for dinner.

Guessing that Leonora would be wearing something dark and sophisticated, she chose a light pink dress dotted with tiny white flowers. It had thin shoulder-straps and a mock elasticated draw-string top. This, in conjunction with a tiny edging of lace at the hem, which ended just above her knee, made it look like a child's dress, and although she put on her cream hold-up stockings and high-heeled strappy sandals, these only served to emphasise the overall effect of youthful freshness. The contrast between her and Leonora would be tremendous, and if she'd read Fabrizio correctly this should serve to increase his desire for her, and enhance their night together.

Although Fabrizio made no comment when she joined them for drinks she saw his eyes widen briefly and felt a moment's triumph. Leonora, wearing black flared trousers with a matching sleeveless tunic, the straps of which divided to meet in a large gold ring just where the bodice covered her breasts, had also run true to form. As Megan talked to the blonde Italian girl she could feel Fabrizio's eyes burning into her. He remained on the other side of the room, apparently deep in discussion with Renato, but Franco joined her and Leonora and a half smile played around his lips as he looked from one girl to the other.

'We should make a film tonight,' he remarked. 'You, Leonora, could play the weary, worldly-wise female who takes the innocent *ingénue* under her wing. As for you Megan, you have cast yourself perfectly into the role of total innocent.'

'It's a warm evening and the dress is comfortable,' said Megan casually.

Franco shook his head. 'I think you've been very clever. Maybe I was wrong about you.'

'In what way?' she asked with interest.

'It's of no importance. Ah, time for dinner I think.'

The maid was standing in the doorway smiling at everyone. When she caught Franco's eye the smile vanished, and Megan saw how she flinched away from the man as he moved past her.

Fabrizio's fingers touched Megan lightly in the middle of her back, where the soft skin was exposed. 'You look as though you're wearing your little sister's dress,' he said huskily.

'I don't have a little sister.'

'What a pity. I might have liked her.'

'I'm afraid you'll have to make do with me,' said Megan, surprised at how bold she was feeling. It was as though the knowledge that Alessandra was away and she and Fabrizio were going to be alone together for the whole night had changed her; that and all the things that had happened to her in this house.

As usual dinner was delicious. They started with gazpacho soup, followed by tender veal cutlets, tiny new potatoes and a tossed green salad, then fresh raspberries and a jug of cream. Megan poured a tiny drop of cream onto her dessert.

'Surely you're not watching your weight?' asked Renato.

Megan laughed. 'No.'

'Then have more cream. There is nothing more sensual than the sensation of cream sliding down the back of your throat, don't you agree Leonora?'

'Not quite. I can think of something that's more sensual,' she said, licking some cream from the corner of her mouth as she spoke. Megan, who hadn't wanted to appear greedy, hastily poured some more over the fruit. It seemed that in this house excess was not the exception but the rule.

After the meal they took their coffee into the large drawing room and there, as Renato, Franco and Leonora chatted, Fabrizio brought out Alessandra's modelling portfolio. 'I thought you might be interested in this,' he said to Megan.

'I'd love to look. How far back do these pictures go?'

'To the beginning of her career. See, isn't she beautiful? The camera adores her.' Megan slowly turned the pages of the album. Alessandra had scarcely changed at all physically, and it was obvious that she showed clothes off to their best advantage. As well as the conventional fashion shots there were other more bizarre ones, in which she was clad in leather, or sitting astride a rocking horse with one hand resting on her knee and the other touching the side of her face with her little finger resting between her pouting lips.

'There isn't a bad picture here,' murmured Megan. 'It must be wonderful to be so beautiful.'

'The good thing about Alessandra is that she doesn't realise how beautiful she is,' said Fabrizio. 'Truly beautiful women can sometimes be obsessed by their looks, which is boring. Alessandra is interested in other things, partly due to my influence I like to think.'

A sudden thought struck Megan and she started to

look through the portfolio again. Although it was true that Alessandra hadn't changed physically, there was a difference in the expression in her eyes. In the early photos the large, violet eyes were clear, open and trusting. They looked like those of a girl who was excited by the prospect of life and anxious to taste its delights. Then the expression changed. She no longer looked so trusting, nor so innocent. The camera had caught something that was not so obvious in the flesh. Alessandra's eyes were now more knowing, but also more guarded. She no longer looked as though she had her whole life ahead of her and relished the thought. She looked as though she'd tasted life and it had altered her.

'What are you looking at?' asked Fabrizio.

'The look in her eyes, it's changed.'

'Of course it's changed. Alessandra's grown up. The look in your eyes has changed already, and it will change even more before you leave here.' Megan felt a tremor run through her and a pulse throbbed in the side of her neck. Fabrizio smiled at her. 'Let us go upstairs,' he said softly. 'I cannot wait any longer.' Megan got hastily to her feet. She glanced at the other three but their heads were together and they continued talking, apparently oblivious to the fact that she and Fabrizio were leaving.

'Goodnight,' she said politely.

Only Leonora bothered to lift her head. 'I hope it is a good one for you,' she remarked, and for a second Megan hesitated, then Fabrizio caught hold of her hand and it was too late. Together they climbed the staircase to the master bedroom.

The room that Fabrizio shared with Alessandra was enormous. Megan had thought that hers was large, but it paled into insignificance next to this. The space was dominated by a huge, antique four-poster bed with a canopy top, and the blue and gold colours of the heavy material reflected in the many tapestries that covered the walls. Most of them depicted couples in exotic sexual positions, and were reproductions from the Kama Sutra and ancient Indian temples.

'Did your uncle collect these tapestries?' she asked curiously, wondering if he too had been a sexual libertine.

'No, they're mine. They're useful in here. They help to muffle the noise.'

As Megan began to realise the significance of what

he was saying a flush stained her cheeks. Fabrizio started to kiss her. Pushing down the thin straps of her dress, his mouth travelled over the sensitive area of her shoulders and collarbone. When their lips met his tongue trailed around the inside of her mouth and gums in long, slow caresses and she gave a sigh of pleasure.

'I adore your dress, it was a brilliant idea,' he murmured and then he picked her up and placed her in the middle of the high bed. He continued kissing and caressing her for a few minutes before peeling off her stockings. Megan closed her eyes, relaxing in the blissful sensuality of it all.

'Raise your arms,' Fabrizio commanded her, 'I want to take your dress off.' Without opening her eyes Megan languidly raised her hands above her head and as the dress was removed she felt the caress of air upon her exposed skin. She sighed again in keen anticipation of remembered pleasures, pleasures that would soon come again.

Her dream was abruptly shattered when her arms were pulled roughly apart and she heard two sharp metallic clicks. Opening her eyes she twisted her head and saw that Fabrizio had fastened her wrists to each of the bed posts. Fear rushed through her. 'Why did you do that?'

'Because I wanted to,' he replied, and now it was her ankles that were being fastened and within a few seconds she was totally helpless, her arms and legs chained to the bed posts, her body entirely naked except for a pair of silk bikini pants.

She watched as Fabrizio removed his own clothes, and at the sight of his lean, muscular body and already impressive erection she began to ache with need. 'This isn't another of your games, is it?' she asked fearfully.

Fabrizio stared down at her, his dark eyes unfathomable. 'How disappointed you look. What did you expect, a night of sex such as Nick might have given you?'

'No, a night like the one we had at the beginning.'

'You were only a novice then. It's different now. Tonight I shall give you orders, orders that I expect to be obeyed. If you fail to obey them you'll be punished.'

'But what about pleasure?' she asked incredulously. 'You said we were going to have a wonderful time.'

'We will have a wonderful time, I promise you. There will be plenty of pleasure for you, and I hope that you will learn to enjoy the punishments as well.'

Megan struggled against her bonds, twisting her arms and legs, but it was pointless. The handcuffs were strong and she knew that it was useless to cry out. There was very little chance of her being heard, Fabrizio had already made that clear. And even if the sound should carry, she doubted that anyone in this household would come to her rescue.

'Relax,' he instructed. 'This is where the pleasure begins.'

He lay down at the foot of the bed, his head between her outstretched thighs and she felt his hands caressing the soft skin at the top of her legs before he picked up a small pair of nail scissors from the floor and carefully cut away her panties. Her body tightened in anticipation and she realised that the feeling of helplessness increased her excitement. Although it was frightening not being able to move, it also heightened her senses, and when Fabrizio's tongue started to stroke upwards against the shaft of her clitoris she uttered a sharp cry of delight.

He wound his left arm around her right thigh, his fingers moving lightly up and down it while he used his right hand to open her up. Her body began to tremble and when she felt the tip of his tongue easing into her vagina her hips jerked, lifting her body off the bed. Immediately he withdrew his tongue and once again licked upwards against the shaft of her throbbing clit, occasionally using the side of his tongue instead.

The tightness in her belly was driving her wild. She could feel her muscles coiling and slithering and her breasts were longing to be touched or licked. She wished she could use her own hands to rub her aching nipples, but she couldn't. She had to rely on Fabrizio for everything.

'You taste delicious,' he whispered as his tongue flicked inside her again, licking away some of the juices that were flowing from her. Megan began to gasp with rising excitement. She was so near to coming that it was painful, and again she moved her hips, desperate to feel the feather-light touch of his tongue swirling on the top of her clitoris, something that she knew would bring about her orgasm instantly.

'I want you to come now,' said Fabrizio, lifting his head from between her thighs for a moment.

'I'm nearly there,' she groaned. 'If you'd just ...'

'I decide what I do. You have to obey me. I expect you to come this time. If you don't you'll be punished.'

For the first time Megan understood what was expected of her during the night.

His tongue moved slowly from her soaking entrance up and down her silky inner lips and caressed the shaft of the clitoris once more. She felt as though her body was swollen to bursting point, all it needed was that one special touch and she'd explode into orgasmic ecstasy, but Fabrizio's tongue stayed away from the top of her frantic little bud. Although she tightened her internal muscles in an attempt to trigger the climax herself, even this additional pressure wasn't sufficient. Blissful release was so near and yet so far that she started to sob at the cruelty of it all.

Then, to her horror, the delicious sensations ceased and Fabrizio lifted his head once more. 'You didn't climax,' he said in apparent astonishment.

'That's because I needed a different touch,' she wailed.

'Are you saying that I'm a poor lover?' he asked with interest.

Megan's head was moving restlessly from side to side, every fibre of her being still ready for the climax that she'd been denied. She could hardly bear to talk to him, but she knew that she had to answer and answer correctly. 'No, of course not.'

'It was your fault, wasn't it?'

'No!' cried Megan.

'The right answer is yes,' said Fabrizio harshly. 'I'll ask you again. It was your fault wasn't it?'

Hoping against hope that if she said yes he'd allow her to come, Megan finally acquiesced. 'Yes,' she whispered.

'Then you were being deliberately difficult and you must be punished.'

'Aren't you going to let me come first?' she cried.

'Of course not. You had your chance, it's time I took you in hand.' Abruptly, he unfastened her, and before she had a chance to resist he lifted her up and carried her across the room, before sitting on a high padded stool and laying her face down across his naked thighs.

'Perhaps after this you'll understand that when I give an order I expect to be obeyed,' he said, and as she felt his hand striking her bottom she gave a scream of astonished disbelief. Ignoring her cries his hand continued to rise and fall, spanking her buttocks until she could feel them glowing with the heat of the blows.

She wriggled desperately against his thighs,

inadvertently stimulating her clitoris so that the heat spread through her belly as well as her buttocks, and once more her treacherous body prepared for an orgasm. 'If you come now the evening is over,' said Fabrizio harshly, and he increased the strength of his blows so that the promised climax ebbed away and she was left squirming and crying.

When he finally stopped she was weeping, not from the pain but from the humiliation of it all. She could see how aroused he was by what had happened. He was fully erect, his cock swollen and purple at the tip while a tiny drop of clear fluid had trickled out of the slit at the top.

'Back to bed I think,' he said and even though she protested and struggled it was easy for him to over-power her. Soon she was lying on the bed once more, her wrists and ankles fastened. She stared up at him, her tear-streaked face flushed with sexual excitement, an excitement that she was ashamed to acknowledge but which had her hips twitching as she waited to see what would happen next.

Having secured her to the bed, Fabrizio moved away leaving her alone and without any form of stimulation. 'I want to give your body time to calm down,' he explained. 'Once it has I shall start touching you, caressing your breasts and belly.' Megan began to tremble. 'The only difference this time is that I don't want you to come,' he continued casually. 'That shouldn't pose too great a problem since you didn't come just now.'

'That was because you wouldn't let me,' she protested.

'It seems you need to learn more about how to control your own sexuality,' he murmured. When he returned to the side of the bed he reached down and the backs of his fingers brushed over her breasts. 'Yes, I think we can begin again.'

It was true that Megan's climax wasn't imminent any more, but as soon as she felt his fingers moving in light, sensuous circular strokes across her abdomen and between her hips and ribs, the hot, tight feeling began once more. Appalled at how quickly her body was reacting she tried to move away from his cruelly insidious caresses, but she was too tightly fastened to allow anything but the slightest movement. She could feel her muscles jumping beneath his fingertips, and when she heard him give a soft laugh she knew that he could feel them too. Sexual tension was rushing through her, tightening every muscle and nerve ending as once more her newly tutored body clamoured for the satisfaction on which it now depended.

Eventually Fabrizio's remorseless hand moved upwards and he began to circle each of her breasts in turn. She groaned with despairing pleasure as they started to swell. 'You love this, don't you?' he remarked, staring deeply into her eyes. 'If you could only see how gorgeous you look, and so different from the day you arrived for the interview wearing that dreadful skirt.'

Megan didn't answer him, she didn't dare because she was frantically trying to subdue her wanton flesh, but when his fingertips started to circle her nipples and she felt them harden, sharp shards of pleasure seared through her body. Then, when he tugged lightly on a nipple, it felt as though it was attached to the back of her clitoris because a corresponding flash of pleasure coursed through her there and she began to utter tiny cries of anticipation.

'Be careful,' Fabrizio warned her. 'Remember, if you come you'll be punished and this time the punishment will be worse.'

'I can't help it,' she cried and to her shame she could feel tears creeping from beneath her closed eyelids.

Fabrizio wiped them away with the back of his hand. 'I adore it when you cry; it's so sexy.'

'Why do you keep tormenting me?' she moaned, as his hand left her breasts and crept down between her spread thighs.

'Because I love watching you struggle as you learn each lesson,' he explained. 'I want to teach you everything there is to know about sex. I promised you that your life would change if you came here, and I always keep my promises.'

When his fingers brushed against her pubic hair Megan cried out in protest. 'Don't touch me there, I know I'll come.'

'Then you must learn to discipline yourself better.'

Megan wished that she could. Her entire body was quaking now. Her hips lifted off the bed, and as he slid a finger inside her she knew that within a few seconds she was going to come. He moved his finger slowly in and out, spreading her own moisture up and down her sex lips, but she was grateful that he avoided touching her clitoris. Then, as his finger re-entered her, he pressed up against the top of her vaginal wall and began to move his fingertip in a firm rotation that produced an entirely new sensation. A heavy, sweet ache filled her vagina, an ache that spread outwards until the tingles of pleasure turned to an insistent pulsating rhythm just behind her clitoris.

'I thought you'd like this,' she heard him say. Then her tormented body exploded into the wickedly delayed climax she'd been longing for and she thrashed helplessly around on the bed, the muscles of her arms and legs pulling against the handcuffs in uncontrollable spasms.

Her cries of joy were tinged with fear and when she finally fell silent she looked into Fabrizio's unforgiving face. 'What a pity, it seems that you'll have to be punished again.'

'I couldn't help it,' she protested.

'You keep saying that. I'm beginning to find it irritating. Let me see, how shall I punish you this time?'

Megan said nothing. She was already afraid and also, she was ashamed to realise, excited. She didn't want to be hurt, even now she could remember how her buttocks had burned when he'd spanked her, but his total control and domination of her was arousing, and she knew that her body was beginning to enjoy the pain as well as the pleasure.

She was released from the handcuffs once more and

this time Fabrizio went over to one of the fitted wardrobes and brought out a strange leather harness which he quickly fitted on to her. Her breasts were encircled by large metallic rings attached to leather strips which fastened tightly behind her back and neck. Her breasts were lifted and thrust forward by the rings and after surveying her for a moment Fabrizio nodded with satisfaction before pulling her hands behind her back and tying them with a silk scarf. Then he took her across to the stool and sat her on it.

'Straighten your back.'

Megan obeyed instantly, and immediately realised that this made her breasts even more prominent. With her arms pulled behind her back it was as though she was thrusting the rounded globes forward provocatively, deliberately trying to excite him when the truth was that she had no choice. Fabrizio had orchestrated the entire scene and it obviously pleased him because again he was fully erect.

'Excellent,' he murmured to himself. 'A perfect target.'

'What do you mean, a target?' cried Megan, but he didn't answer her. Instead he opened a drawer in one of the bedside tables and pulled out a thin leather whip.

Walking back to Megan he pulled the whip thought-fully through the fingers of his left hand and then laid it gently across the tops of her breasts in a caress that made her shiver. 'I don't expect you to keep silent during this,' he told her. 'In fact I'll be amazed if you do.' And as she gazed uncomprehendingly at him, he flicked his wrist and the gentle caress turned into a sharp, stinging blow that left a thin red line across her throbbing flesh.

Megan screamed with shock, then cried out as the pain increased, climbing steadily to a peak before eventually dying away. She didn't even have time to utter a protest before he flicked his wrist again and once more the blood rushed to the abused area. Megan began to cry in earnest now. Every time the whip fell the pain intensified and he didn't wait for it to die away but allowed blow after blow to fall.

The strikes weren't heavy, the skin was never broken, and as he continued to punish her she realised that her breasts were feeling hot and engorged, causing the metal rings to bite deeply into them.

Now she wasn't simply experiencing pain but pleasure too, an extraordinarily heightened pleasure as her breast tissue flushed, suffused with the blood rushing through her veins. When she tried to move on the stool she felt the tell-tale dampness between her thighs. This dreadful punishment, something she had never imagined anyone doing to her, was turning her on. When he finally threw the whip away the ache between her thighs was so bad that she somehow found the courage to express her need.

'Please touch me,' she begged Fabrizio.

Roughly, he pulled her off the stool, manhandled her over to the bed and pushed her backwards. Thrusting a hand between her thighs, his fingers quickly located her clitoris. This time he touched her where she most enjoyed it and with humiliating speed she was engulfed by an intense rush of pleasure.

'Well well,' said Fabrizio. 'It seems that wasn't quite the punishment I'd intended.'

'It hurt,' cried Megan.

'Of course it hurt, but look what else it did to you.' Pulling her to her feet he walked her across the room and forced her to stand in front of the full-length mirror in one of the wardrobe doors. She looked flushed, sated and utterly wanton. Unable to believe what she was seeing she closed her eyes and heard him laugh. 'You see, I promised that you'd be different by the time you left here. Now you can see for yourself that you already are.'

'Is that all for tonight?' she whispered.

'No. There is one more command I have for you,' he replied.

She was shocked to realise that she was pleased.

Chapter Nine

Fabrizio looked at Megan as she sat on the edge of the bed, her hands still fastened behind her back and her eyes wide with a mixture of anxiety and fear. Her confusion at what was happening to her was exciting him more than he'd expected. She was such a quick learner, and at the same time deliciously ashamed of her own responses. Remembering how Renato had doubted him Fabrizio felt even more content.

Strangely, he wasn't as anxious for Alessandra's return as he'd expected. He knew that she'd want to know everything that had gone on tonight, but the prospect of sharing it with her didn't appeal to him. He knew that it was his fault but she'd become too accepting of all that happened. When he related tonight's events, he doubted if she'd find them as exciting as he had. Then again, Megan was new and he understood himself well enough to know that for him novelty was everything. No doubt by the time her six months were up he'd be bored with her, and Alessandra would once more become the main focus of his sex life.

'Do you want to know what my third command is?' he asked the waiting girl. He was pleased when she nodded rather than spoke. This was what he enjoyed, the fear and subservience that she was showing coupled with the incredible pleasure that she was learning to enjoy. 'You see this clock,' he continued, indicating the marble mantelpiece over the antique fireplace. Again Megan nodded. 'As you can see the second hand is large, which enables me to judge time very accurately. You will have two minutes in which to bring me to a climax using your mouth.' He saw the look of apprehension in her eyes and it pleased him. 'I know that this isn't something you're particularly proficient at, but given the circumstances it shouldn't be too hard a task for you. Here, let me untie you.'

Now Fabrizio sat on the side of the bed and Megan hastily fell to her knees, resting her small hands on his thighs. When she began to bend her head towards his erection he felt her soft brown curls tickling the skin at the sides of his belly. His muscles tensed and trembled and he knew then that it would take all his self-control to defeat her. The problem was, he was too excited. Watching her endure her punishment, weeping even as she climaxed, had him aching with need. Yet somehow he must control himself sufficiently to make sure that she failed one more time.

'Am I allowed to use my hands at all?' she asked anxiously.

'To position me correctly yes, but not to stimulate me. The clock starts now.'

Megan's tongue moved awkwardly along the shaft of his penis and the fact that she was so unskilled at what she was doing nearly made him come. He was used to Alessandra's knowing ways, and the difference was highly arousing. 'I don't think you're trying hard enough,' he said harshly, trying to break his train of thought and make what was happening less dangerously erotic.

Megan quickly took the base of his penis in one hand and then started to lick upwards, first on one side and then on the other. Fabrizio felt his testicles tighten and draw upwards. There was a hot tingling sensation at the base of his shaft, a certain warning that his climax was imminent, but he breathed slowly and deeply, watching the clock in yet another attempt at distraction.

The hands seemed to be moving very slowly and now he had every reason to be grateful for Megan's lack of experience. As she grew bolder she took his glans between her lips and slid her mouth slowly down the shaft and back again, carefully covering her teeth with her lips so as not to cause him any discomfort. Fabrizio smiled to himself. If she had but known it, the scratch of her teeth against his delicate tissue would have triggered a climax immediately.

'You have twenty seconds to go,' he informed her. 'I should warn you now that you will not enjoy the punishment failure will bring.'

He stared down at Megan as, in a last desperate attempt to make him spill his seed, she flicked her tongue lightly across the ridge on the underside of his penis. Fabrizio's body stiffened and he bit hard on his lower lip. This light touch, like the caress of a butterfly's wings, was unbearably exciting and he knew that if she continued for a few seconds more he would come. Glancing at the clock again he was relieved to see that she'd stumbled on the right move just seconds too late.

'Your time's up,' he said, and to his own ears his voice sounded thick with lust, although he guessed that Megan would only hear the words and not the way in which they were said. Apparently not hearing him at all she continued with what she was doing and he longed to allow her to finish the job but knew that he mustn't. Fiercely he caught hold of her hair, jerking her head up and back and she stared at him, her expression horrified.

'You're going to punish me again aren't you?'

'Of course. You failed, and the task was really very simple.'

'You nearly came, I know you did,' she protested.

'Nearly isn't good enough. Stand up. I have to get you prepared for your punishment.'

As he moved backwards and forwards to the bed, carrying the various items that were necessary, Fabrizio made sure that from time to time his arm or fingers brushed against Megan's bare skin. Every time he did this she would tremble violently. Her eyes followed him around the room, growing more and more apprehensive with everything she saw. Finally he was ready.

'Over here,' he instructed her, but to his surprise she remained standing in the middle of the room. 'Didn't you hear what I said?' he asked dangerously.

'I don't think I want to do this,' whispered Megan.

Fabrizio looked hard at her. 'Of course you do. The only problem with you is that you're ashamed to admit my punishments turn you on. There's no need to feel ashamed. Sexual satisfaction can be arrived at in many ways, and these are some of them. You're naturally submissive. You're turned on by everything I do. After tonight, I shall introduce you to a different world, where for a time you will be in a position of power. Then you will have the opportunity to discover which particular scenario appeals to you most. For myself, I suspect that this is where your true talent lies. Now, no more of your nonsense. Come, you took part in the test and you failed. It's too late to back out now.'

Still Megan didn't move and Fabrizio had to pull her across the room and lie her widthways across the bed. Beneath her belly and upper thighs he placed a folded bolster, and because the bed was so wide this meant that she was fully supported, with her buttocks raised high in the air. Lying face down on the bed she began to twist and turn, and he knew that she'd guessed what was coming.

'I told you yesterday that soon I would be spilling myself inside you here,' he reminded her, his hands caressing the softly rounded cheeks of her bottom. 'As long as you relax there will be pleasure, after a little pain of course.'

The words were deliberate and Megan began to whimper in protest. Fabrizio flicked at her buttocks with the backs of his fingers. 'Be quiet, save your whimpering for later.' He was so hard now that it was painful for him but still he proceeded slowly, anxious to make the punishment memorable not simply for the pain but also for the incredible dark pleasure that she would receive.

He began by massaging the whole of her back with scented oil, his fingers pressing firmly on the tight muscles beneath the skin until he felt her start to relax. Occasionally he slid a hand beneath her and his oiled fingers lightly caressed her rapidly hardening nipples. Every time he did this she murmured with pleasure and relaxed even more.

It was only when he spread her buttocks apart and poured the oil into the crevice, watching the cool liquid flow down over the tight, puckered opening and then beneath, to where he knew her vulva would be swollen and throbbing, that she started to protest. He ignored her cries. He was now so caught up in the excitement of it all that nothing she said or did would have stopped him.

He began by inserting two fingers inside her rectum. Even this intrusion made her utter a cry of protest, which continued as he moved them around, gradually stretching her until he was able to add a third. The three fingers moved slowly and carefully, touching the sensitive walls and pressing on vital nerve endings until her moans of discomfort changed and she began to move her upper body restlessly against the bed.

Realising that she was already becoming excited he removed his fingers and at last was able to start pressing the bulbous head of his massive erection against her. This time Megan's cry of protest was far louder and he stopped for a moment. His hands, which were gripping her hips, released her and he covered his penis with lubricating jelly. Even so, as he started to ease himself inside her she grew frantic with terror.

'No, please don't,' she exclaimed. 'You're too large, and it hurts me.'

'It isn't pain, *cara*,' he whispered seductively. 'Think of it as a different kind of pleasure. Isn't your belly aching? Aren't you hot between your thighs?'

'Yes, yes,' admitted Megan, 'but you're too big.'

'You have to relax and let me in,' he explained, but her muscles remained tight and although he pulled on her hips, trying to force his way past the ridge of muscle around the entrance, he couldn't. Whilst continuing to sob Megan was pressing her breasts against the bed, and he saw one of her hands move beneath her to try and touch her own belly.

Quickly he slid a hand under her, but lower down, and to his delight he found that she was very damp between her thighs. His fingers glided over the slippery flesh until he found her clitoris and as he stroked the side of the shaft she began to tremble violently. Taking advantage of this he thrust heavily forward into her and after Megan's initial scream she fell silent as he remained motionless, allowing her body time to absorb the strange full sensation that he knew would be frightening for her.

Eventually her sobbing stopped but she continued to

move her upper body around restlessly. 'The worst is over now,' he told her. 'When I start to move again there will be more pleasure than pain.'

'Why does there have to be any pain?' she asked in bewilderment.

'For two reasons. First, because you're being punished,' and as he said this he started to move around inside her and heard her groan in response. 'Second, because you love it, and it's time you admitted that.'

'I don't! I don't!' she retorted, but when his hand moved to her vulva again, her swollen sex lips and erect clitoris told a different story.

'What a liar you are,' he laughed, and now his fingers were working between her thighs while he moved his hips in a short, sharp rhythm. She was so tight, the muscles so firmly clasped around him, that it was difficult for him not to come immediately. He heard himself gasping and when the tingling in his testicles moved upwards through the shaft of his penis he knew that he could hold back no longer.

Megan was uttering strange guttural sounds, half out of her mind with the sensations surging through her, but Fabrizio couldn't think about her pleasure. The hot tightness of her rectum combined with the fact that she was lying beneath him like this, submissive, humiliated and taking pleasure from such an act of decadence, was enough for him. A few seconds later his head went back and with a roar of triumph he spilled himself into her as a deliciously intense orgasm flooded through his body, leaving him weak and shaken by the strength of it.

When he'd recovered a little he realised that Megan was moving restlessly, whimpering in despair, and he knew that she still hadn't come. 'Tighten the muscles around me, keep me inside you,' he whispered, knowing that this would also increase the pressure in the whole of her pelvic area. He felt her obey, felt his soft, sensitive flesh gripped even tighter, and then he skimmed his finger across the head of her clitoris while at the same time trapping her left nipple cruelly between the thumb and finger of his left hand. It was this final flash of red-hot pain that allowed Megan's body to spasm in an ecstasy of release. For several minutes she shook beneath him and he felt her muscles pulsating in uncontrollable contractions until at last her orgasm died away.

Afterwards Megan remained slumped over the bolster until Fabrizio pulled her off it, and for a moment they lay quietly together, her head resting against his chest. Suddenly her eyes opened and she stared at him. 'I'm afraid,' she confessed.

Fabrizio's heart began to race. 'Afraid of what?'

'Where this is going to end.'

'Live always for the moment, that is what I do. It is time for me to sleep now I think.'

Megan's expression changed to one of surprise. 'Aren't I staying here with you?'

'Of course, but you will not be sleeping with me.'

'What do you mean?'

Fabrizio didn't explain. Instead he pulled her off the bed and, despite her protests, stood her on the carpet and tied her to the bed-post so that she was facing the mirror in the wardrobe door, a mirror that he could see when he was lying in bed.

He saw her look at herself and flinch at the image that she presented. She was still in the body harness and all at once Fabrizio had a delicious idea. 'I want you to enjoy the night,' he said with a smile. 'Spread your legs for me.'

'No,' protested Megan, keeping her ankles firmly together. With a sigh of irritation Fabrizio wrenched them apart and then fastened a spreader-board between them. This meant that it was easy for him to slip three smooth ivory balls inside her that vibrated when warm. He knew how hot she must be inside, how her still excited flesh would soon start the vibrations, and he watched her face carefully. Within less than a minute her lips parted in surprise and a tiny 'Oh!' escaped.

'Does that feel good?' he enquired with mock solicitousness.

'Yes, but I don't want them to keep moving all night. I'm exhausted. How will I sleep?'

'It's up to you. The more excited you become the more the balls will vibrate. I think there is just one finishing touch needed and then I can go to bed.' With that he put a wide, black leather belt around her waist. From the centre there hung a strap which he fastened between her legs and up to the other side. This meant that there was continuous pressure on her vulva, pressure that would keep her excited; this excitement would engender warmth which in turn would make sure that the ivory balls kept moving.

'There, you can come as many times as you like while I sleep.'

'I don't want to come any more,' said Megan despairingly.

'Then learn to ignore the sensations. This might actually help to train you, although primarily it's intended for pleasure.'

'Yours or mine?'

'Why, both of course.' Then Fabrizio slid beneath the fresh silk sheets that were placed on the bed every day, turned on his side and fell asleep.

He woke at regular intervals during the night and each time he switched on the light above the mirror so that he could see Megan's reflection there. Often she was spasming, her body shaken by what were clearly painful tremors of ecstasy as her exhausted body was forced to climax time after time by the insidious titillation of the device inside her. Once or twice she cried out to him, begging him to release her, but each time he merely turned off the light and returned to sleep.

At five in the morning he woke as daylight came in through the curtains. Climbing out of bed he stood in front of Megan who was slumped exhausted against the bed-post, her eyelids drooping, her breasts still engorged, and as he ran a hand between her thighs and her eyes flew open he felt the tell-tale stickiness that revealed she was in a state of arousal.

'Did you have an enjoyable night?' he asked.

'I can't come any more,' she sobbed.

'Then that's good. At last you are sated. You have time for a couple of hours sleep before you need to start work.'

'I haven't been able to come for the last hour,' she continued, tears rolling down her face.

'Why does that matter?'

'Because I wanted to,' she shouted, and now there was anger in her voice, anger which made his blood race because this was when it became exciting, when someone naturally submissive and docile was pushed to the point at which they began to fight back and revealed fresh aspects of themselves. 'Don't you understand?' she continued. 'These balls that you've put inside me have kept me on the edge even though I can't come, and it hurts. My breasts are aching and so is my stomach.'

'Perhaps you need a little more stimulation for one final climax,' he suggested.

Megan shook her head. 'No! I couldn't. Really I couldn't. Please, let me go now. I must get some sleep.'

'But you want to come don't you?' he asked tenderly, his hands caressing the sides of her face and then he began kissing her and he felt her body respond. Her breasts pressed against his chest, her hips moved as far from the bed-post as they could, and she groaned with despairing desire. Taking pity on her he knelt on the ground and allowed his tongue to work its magic so that at last, after a frantic, frustrated hour, she shook gently from head to toe in a final spasm of release that left her sobbing with gratitude.

'Today you will have a day off,' said Fabrizio, as he untied her and removed the harness and the strap between her legs before getting her to bear down so that he could remove the vibrating balls. 'The following day, as I mentioned late last night, you will have an opportunity to experience something entirely new. I will be interested to see your reaction to it.'

'I can't believe I'm allowing all this to happen,' she murmured.

'You aren't allowing it to happen,' pointed out Fabrizio. 'You're an active participant in this, Megan. You may deny it to yourself if you will, but that's the truth, and it's a truth that one day you'll have to face.'

The following afternoon Alessandra finally arrived back from Milan. Quickly she changed into a tight, thin-strapped cotton top and a skimpy pair of shorts that accentuated her long, brown legs, before going out to the patio at the back of the house. There she sprawled elegantly on the garden swing-seat and looked over to where Fabrizio was standing by the water feature, watching the fountain cascade over the multi-coloured pebbles.

'It makes a lovely sound doesn't it?' he remarked idly.

'Very restful,' agreed Alessandra. She was anxious to know what had happened in her absence and had fully expected Fabrizio to pick her up at the airport with details of how he'd got on while alone with Megan. When he'd called her on her mobile saying that he was too busy, alarm bells had begun to ring in her head.

Now, as he kept his back carefully turned to her, the alarm bells sounded again. Obviously he wasn't as anxious as she was to talk about it, which could only mean one thing: Fabrizio was becoming involved with Megan. She was no longer a toy for them all to play with, part of a game in which they were all involved. Instead, probably entirely by accident, the girl was affecting Fabrizio on a personal level and Alessandra knew that this meant danger for herself.

'Tell me what happened while I was away,' she murmured.

'Not a lot.'

'Didn't you spend a night alone with Megan?'

For the first time Fabrizio turned to look at her. 'I like the outfit.'

Alessandra nodded. She was always totally immune to compliments about her appearance, and right now they were the last thing she was interested in hearing. 'Why won't you tell me?'

'It wasn't particularly interesting,' replied Fabrizio.

Alessandra raised her eyebrows. 'It must have been. Unless the pair of you spent a pleasant night in each other's arms making love in the missionary position, and billing and cooing like a pair of doves.'

'My, my, the claws are out this afternoon, aren't they!' said Fabrizio with a smile.

'Not really, but I think you're behaving rather badly. Megan's meant to be an amusement for all of us. Why are you keeping her to yourself?'

'We played commands and punishments,' said Fabrizio. 'Satisfied?'

Alessandra's eyes brightened. 'Of course I'm not satisfied. Tell me the details. What did you make her do? And how did she behave when you punished her?'

'One question at a time! I asked her to climax on

command, which she failed to do. Then, after she'd been punished, I ordered her not to come but she did. Finally I gave her a time limit to give me a climax, using her mouth.'

'Did she succeed?'

'No, she failed with all of my instructions.'

Alessandra couldn't keep the excitement out of her voice. 'You had to punish her a lot then?'

Fabrizio gave a lazy smile. 'Yes I did.'

'And how did she react to that?'

'She resisted, not much at first but quite a lot later on. It was very arousing.'

'So I can see,' said Alessandra softly as she saw the tell-tale bulge in his trousers. 'Obviously just the memory of it is sufficient to excite you. So, has she lost her nerve yet? Does she want to go back to Lincoln-shire?'

'Not at all. I think the most delicious thing that happened last night was watching her struggle to come to terms with the fact that she was enjoying the pun-ishments. Of course, at first the pain distressed her, but she quickly learnt how stimulating pain can be, and also how exciting it is to allow yourself to be humili-ated and controlled.'

'Were the two of you alone all night?' asked Alessandra, secretly horrified at the way in which Fabrizio was relishing re-living the memories of what had happened.

'Yes, I thought it important that we had some time alone before the rest of you were let loose on her. At least now she's a little more prepared.'

'Did you do that for our sakes, or to protect her?'

'For everyone's sake. None of us will benefit if she panics and leaves. I hope you're not getting jealous, Alessandra. That would be very tiresome.'

'I'm not jealous, but I don't think you're playing by the rules.'

'It's my game, I make up the rules.'

Alessandra shook her head. 'That isn't true. We all discussed Megan coming here, and we all had to approve her selection. Admittedly it was your idea, but then you always have the best ideas. Just the same, we're all involved. If you want her to yourself then admit it, but stop pretending it's a game in which we're all having fun.'

'I think you must be suffering from jet-lag,' said Fabrizio smoothly. 'Why don't you go and have a lie down?'

'I'm not suffering from jet-lag. What's the matter, don't you like hearing the truth?'

For a moment Fabrizio looked so angry that Alessandra panicked. Then he shrugged, which in turn made her angry. It was as though she was of no account. 'Maybe you're right,' he said. 'Tomorrow she'll be watching Leonora and Renato. If you like you can join us.'

'If she's with Leonora and Renato, why will you be there?'

'Because I'm taking her as an observer. Leonora will be busy, as will Renato, although he probably won't be as busy as Leonora!' He laughed.

'I'd like to be there,' said Alessandra swiftly.

'Then you'll have to ask me nicely,' said Fabrizio, and now his dark eyes held a look of desire that she recognised. Her heart began to race. This was what she was afraid of losing: his interest, the sheer overwhelming sexuality of their couplings and the skilful feel of his hands on her body. It was true that occasionally there were moments when she resented his need to totally dominate her, but these moments always passed when the delicious pleasure engulfed her.

'How do I do that?' she asked him with mock innocence.

'Let's go up to the bedroom and see if you can think of something,' suggested Fabrizio.

With an inward sigh of relief and feeling that, for the moment at least, the danger had passed, Alessandra agreed. All the same, she decided that from now on she'd be more alert to the possibility that Megan might pose a threat to her position as Fabrizio's permanent mistress.

'Did you have a nice trip?' Megan asked Alessandra, as they all sat down to dinner that evening.

Alessandra nodded. 'It went well. The shoot was an easy one. I like the cameraman, he doesn't make ridiculous demands.'

'How disappointing,' laughed Renato. 'I would have thought you'd relish commands, however outlandish.'

'Not in my professional life,' retorted Alessandra, shaking her head and pushing her long hair behind her ears.

As she did this Megan noticed that there were red marks around her wrists and two tiny purple bruises at the base of her throat. Her stomach tightened as she realised that while she'd been working in the library Fabrizio had been giving Alessandra the kind of pleasure that he'd given her the night before. Although she was totally exhausted and knew that she couldn't possibly have faced another session with him herself that day, Megan was surprised to realise that she felt jealous. She knew that she had no right. Alessandra was Fabrizio's mistress; she was merely an employee. Unfortunately, where obsession was concerned, logic didn't seem to help.

She had begun to feel that Fabrizio was hers, that the strange, tortuous pleasure he was inflicting on her was special. It was an unpleasant shock to realise that he was doing exactly the same thing to another woman within a few hours of doing it to her.

'You seem tired,' said Leonora, looking across at Megan. Her tone was sympathetic but her eyes were mischievous. 'I hope you haven't been overdoing it.'

'What do you mean?' asked Megan.

'In the library of course. What else could I mean?'

'I am a little tired,' admitted Megan.

Renato smiled at her. 'Did you have a rough night?' he asked gently. 'You've got very dark shadows under your eyes.'

'I didn't get much sleep,' she admitted.

'Then you must go to bed early tonight,' said

Renato. 'The rest of us are all going to a party at a friend's house so the house will be quiet for you.'

'Are you?' asked Megan in surprise.

Fabrizio looked down the table at her. 'Yes, why are you surprised? Did you want to come? I'm sure it could be arranged with our host and hostess.'

'I don't think it could at this late notice,' said Alessandra sharply. 'Anyway, Megan isn't qualified for that kind of party.'

'What kind of party?' asked Megan.

'It's a themed party for like-minded people,' said Franco, but his reply left Megan none the wiser.

'I think you're right Alessandra,' said Fabrizio. 'Megan isn't yet ready for a party like that. Besides, as Renato says, she needs her beauty sleep. Tomorrow we will try and amuse you ourselves, little Megan.'

'I hope you're not getting bored here?' asked Franco. 'You could always go home to visit your friends next weekend. You haven't left here once yet.'

'I'm fine,' said Megan hastily. The last thing on earth she wanted to do right now was leave Fabrizio. 'I'm very happy here.'

Franco bent his head close to hers. 'Remember, Megan, you – like me – are only an employee. The other four can play with us, amuse themselves with us, make us feel that we belong and then discard us as children discard their toys once they're bored with them. Do not allow yourself to think that you're more important to them than you are.'

Megan didn't reply, but little as she liked the man she knew that he was right. 'I hope you all have a good time,' she said brightly, and as soon as coffee was over she withdrew to the privacy of her room. She quickly fell into a deep sleep and didn't wake until eight the next morning.

Chapter Ten

Megan worked in the library all the following day. She was at last beginning to instil some order, which pleased her. What pleased her even more, however, was the prospect of the exciting evening to come.

Yet much to her dismay, no further mention of anything happening was made and eventually, at eleven o'clock, she retired to bed. She wondered if this was yet another form of torture that Fabrizio was inflicting on her, promising her new delights only to let her down. If so, she didn't like it.

Her body felt restless, her skin extra sensitive because she was longing for some kind of sexual satisfaction. This need for sex was beginning to worry her.

It was as though, because of Fabrizio and the rest of his household, she had become obsessed with her own sexual gratification. It was difficult to believe that she'd once been content with the fleeting attentions of Nick over a weekend. As for the future, she didn't dare to think about that.

It was nearly one o'clock before she finally fell into a restless sleep. At two she was abruptly woken by Alessandra shaking her shoulder. 'Quick, get up,' said Fabrizio's mistress. 'We're taking you upstairs now, only you must be quiet.'

'I don't understand,' mumbled Megan, rubbing the sleep from her eyes. 'What's happening?'

'Don't ask questions,' said Alessandra. 'Just put on a robe and follow me. Fabrizio's already waiting for us.'

Megan stumbled sleepily out of the bedroom, tying the sash of her ankle-length robe as she went. 'It's down on the second floor,' explained Alessandra. 'We're going to watch Leonora and Renato. Only you have to keep very quiet because Renato doesn't know that we're joining them.'

'Does Leonora know?' asked Megan.

Alessandra laughed. 'Naturally. Leonora hates surprises, but she adores an audience. She should excel herself tonight. I only hope Renato appreciates it,' she added thoughtfully.

'Appreciates what?'

'Wait a few minutes and you'll see. Fabrizio, here she is. Can we go in now?'

Fabrizio nodded. 'Leonora's tapped on the inside of the door, which was the pre-arranged signal. That means she's already covered Renato's eyes and ears, but we must still keep quiet. He won't be able to see anything but he would hear a loud noise. The cloth that she ties around his face only muffles sounds. Remember that, Megan, as you watch. Keep your reactions as quiet as possible.'

Fabrizio and Alessandra were on either side of Megan, and as Fabrizio slowly pushed the door open they bundled her into the room, each of them gripping one arm firmly. Both of them also caressed her through her robe and nightdress, each cupping one of her breasts. Fabrizio tweaked her left nipple hard. She felt a sudden searing pain and had to bite her lower lip hard to stop herself from making a sound.

'Well done,' he whispered in her ear. 'Now I know you can keep quiet.'

The room was dimly lit, but it was easy for Megan to

see what was happening. Renato was kneeling in the middle of the room. A black blindfold covered his eyes and ears, and around his neck there was a black leather collar. His hands were tied behind his back with a leather strap and he was motionless as Leonora stood over him.

Leonora herself was wearing black leather boots that nearly reached the tops of her thighs, and there was only a tiny gap between the boots and the hem of her tight-fitting black leather mini-skirt. The only clothing that she had on her upper body was a see-through black lace camisole that was tucked into the waistband of the mini-skirt. The shoulder-straps on the camisole were very thin and Leonora's full breasts were visible to Megan and the other onlookers, but not to the blind-folded Renato kneeling at her feet.

Megan had a strange feeling in the pit of her stom-ach. She'd never seen a man tied up like this, had never imagined someone like Renato being humiliated in such a way, and she wondered what it must feel like to be Leonora. Fabrizio's sister was holding a riding crop in her right hand and as Megan watched she placed it behind Renato's neck, moving it slowly back and forth.

'You know that you're my slave for the night, don't

you?' she asked him. He nodded. Megan wondered if he was forbidden to speak. 'I thought that I commanded you not to grow hard,' continued the blonde girl, as the crop was pulled back and forth over the nape of his neck. 'It seems that you have trouble obeying orders. Sadly I shall have to punish you.'

She didn't sound the least bit sad; in fact she sounded triumphant. Withdrawing the crop, she pushed Renato in the middle of the chest so that he fell awkwardly onto his side, his hands still tethered behind him. Now Megan could see how hard he was, how tight his testicles, and how the thick blue veins throbbed along the shaft of his penis. He looked ready to come at any moment, and as Leonora flicked at the side of his belly with her crop his penis jerked violently.

Now Leonora bent over him, her hands moving swiftly over the throbbing erection. Megan heard Renato moan in terror and guessed that he was afraid of climaxing. Fabrizio put his mouth against Megan's ear. 'She's putting a leather strap on him,' he whispered softly 'It fastens behind his testicles and means that he can't lose his erection. It will make him even more nervous of coming,' he added. Megan was horrified, but at the same time intensely excited.

Having fastened the straps securely, Leonora ordered Renato back on to his knees and then stood in front of him with her legs apart. 'Suck my pussy,' she said. 'Eat me until I come.'

Megan could hear the soft sounds of Renato's mouth working busily between his lover's thighs, could see his head bobbing frantically beneath the hem of the leather skirt, and as Leonora began to tremble Megan started to tremble too. She felt Alessandra's hands untying the sash of her robe, and she didn't protest because she wanted her flesh to be available, to be touched by Fabrizio as she watched the extraordinary scene unfolding in front of her. It was Alessandra though who removed the night-dress as well, and then lightly stroked the other girl's breasts until Megan felt like groaning herself. Eventually Alessandra's hands left her breasts, only to move between her thighs where they encountered the tell-tale stickiness of Megan's excitement.

Megan shook all the more when, in front of her, Leonora's body went rigid before spasming in a delicious climax.

'You took too long,' Leonora announced, the moment the last ripple of pleasure had died away. 'Put your head to the floor.'

Megan watched as Renato, still kneeling, bent from the waist until his forehead was touching the ground. He was totally unable to defend himself and as Leonora moved behind him, her riding crop lifted high in the air, he uttered a choked cry. 'Don't strike me,' he begged her.

'Why not?' she challenged him. 'Can't you control yourself? Are you so pathetic that the touch of my crop will make you come?'

'For God's sake, Leonora, I can't stand any more,' he cried. 'I feel as though I'm going to explode.'

'Perhaps this will change your mind,' said Leonora, and she began to strike each of his buttocks in turn with the riding crop, using alternate backhand and forehand strokes. Renato cried out in pain but Megan could tell that the riding crop was only heightening his sexual tension, bringing him close to the point of no return.

There was a hot, heavy feeling in the pit of Megan's stomach, partly the usual sweet ache of an impending climax and partly something else, something strange that she'd never experienced before. She shifted uncomfortably from one foot to the other until Alessandra turned her head and gave her a warning glance. 'What's the matter?' whispered the model.

'I think I need the bathroom,' explained Megan.

Fabrizio smiled. 'Good, that will make things even better for you,' he whispered, and now Renato turned his head a little. Clearly he'd heard something and as Leonora shot a look of anger at her brother, Fabrizio fell silent.

Apparently tiring of striking her lover, Leonora let her arm hang by her side for a moment, her fingers gripping the end of the crop tightly, almost caressing it and paying particular attention to the rounded end. After a few seconds she bent forward from the waist and Megan watched in horror as the pretty blonde girl deftly began to insert the narrow handle between her lover's buttocks.

Renato cried out in anguish. 'That's not fair. You know I'll come. You're going too far, Leonora.'

'But you love it don't you?' Leonora taunted him. 'You're so hard, so excited. You never experienced anything like this before you met me.' As she spoke she was turning her hand, rotating it clockwise and anticlockwise, sliding the bulbous head deeper inside the still kneeling Renato.

After what had happened to her the previous night, Megan could imagine what it must feel like. In addition she remembered reading that men have a very sensitive gland deep inside the rectum, a gland that when massaged, rapidly precipitates a climax. She could tell that this was true from the way that Renato groaned and writhed in an agony of rising passion as he fought frantically to prevent his pleasure from spilling over.

Her skin felt as though it was stretched too tightly over Megan's stomach. The whole of her insides felt over-full, and the heaviness behind her clitoris was emphasised by the uncomfortable feeling in her bladder. She shifted from one foot to the other, unable to tear her eyes away from what was happening and yet so excited by it that she was terrified she was going to lose control of herself. Renato's cries reached an even greater pitch and Leonora pulled his head up off the floor so that he was now kneeling upright, with the riding crop still being pushed between his buttocks.

Megan could see for herself how close he was to coming. He looked like she felt: ready to explode. As he groaned and begged for mercy Megan realised that she was losing her own battle for control. For a terrible moment she thought that she was going to pee and had to cover her mouth with her hand in order to suppress her groans.

Fabrizio and Alessandra closed in on her. Their hands roamed all over her body, but it was Fabrizio who applied the cruel pressure to her lower belly, apparently not realising the problems that Megan was having.

She began to twist and turn, attempting to avoid his probing fingers because she was so afraid of disgracing herself, and all the time Renato's cries grew in volume until, with a strangled scream, he came. His hips jerked furiously and his seed spilled out of him in bursts. As his body shook, Leonora continued pressing the crop handle deep inside him.

Finally Renato's body was still. His head went back and his mouth opened as he gasped for breath. Megan wondered what he would feel like if he knew that the whole scene had been watched by her and the other two. It would be difficult in the future to think of Renato in the same way, having seen what he'd allowed Leonora to do to him. She couldn't imagine doing anything like it herself, but at the same time was incredibly turned on by it all.

Fabrizio was evidently equally turned on. As he stood behind her, his arms around her waist she felt his erection pressing through the fabric of his slacks and then, almost before she realised what was happening, he'd pushed her down on to the bedroom floor, putting one hand over her mouth as a reminder that she must remain silent.

She felt as though she was on fire between her thighs.

Her buttocks moved against the carpet and even this soft, slightly prickling touch was enough to inflame her. Fabrizio lay next to her and continued his casually cruel massage of her lower belly, pressing hard into the soft tissue so that it was all she could do to keep quiet. As he worked on her, Alessandra knelt on the floor until her head was between Megan's thighs, and as she parted the girl's swollen sex lips and her cool tongue caressed the warm flesh, Megan thought she'd go out of her mind with pleasure.

Fabrizio and Alessandra worked in swift silence, their skill so great that within seconds Megan's body was spiralling upwards. When the heel of Fabrizio's hand pressed against her pubic bone at the same time as Alessandra sucked on her pulsating clit, she came. The incredibly intense contractions gave her blissful release, but as the last tremors died away and her muscles started to relax, Alessandra swept the tip of her tongue in a feather-light caress over the entrance to Megan's urethra and finally she lost control of her bladder, the hot flooding release causing her to weep in silent humiliation.

To Megan's surprise neither Fabrizio nor Alessandra made any comment on what had happened, nor did they give any sign that it was unusual. In fact, Fabrizio seemed pleased and his hand moved over her now relaxed belly, stroking the soft skin tenderly. She knew that he couldn't speak because of Renato, but she felt closer to him than at any other time, because she sensed that what had happened had pleased him.

Turning her head languidly on the floor she saw that Renato was now crouched at Leonora's feet as she sat in one of the bedroom chairs. 'You're useless!' she sneered at him, and presumably because she realised he wouldn't be able to hear her properly she emphasised her words by placing the stiletto heel of her boot just above his belly-button, pressing hard until he winced with pain. 'I let you get away with too much,' she continued. 'Since you're so anxious to climax, perhaps you should come again, and quickly.'

Renato tried to move away from his lover but she caught hold of his hair. 'There, that really frightens you doesn't it? Well it's what you deserve and it's what's going to happen.'

'That's enough for one evening, Leonora,' said Renato.

'How dare you speak to me like that? Have you forgotten who you are?'

'I've had enough of this game,' he continued.

'Well I haven't, and neither's Megan.'

'What?'

'That's right, the demure little English girl's been watching you all this time. There, what do you think of that?'

Renato began turning his head blindly in all directions, trying to locate the exact spot where Megan was watching. Megan shrank back a little but Fabrizio and Alessandra were right behind her, pushing her towards Leonora.

'I don't want to join in,' whispered Megan.

'I want you to,' said Fabrizio. 'I promised that you'd have a chance to see what it was like to dominate. Here's your opportunity.'

'I can't,' she protested.

'Don't do anything you don't want to do,' Renato told Megan. 'Believe me, I know where that can lead to.'

Leonora struck him with the crop. 'Be silent. Here Megan, you can help me make him hard again.'

'You'll have to wait,' protested Renato. 'This is getting beyond a joke, Leonora.'

'Who said anything about joking? Kneel with your forehead on the carpet again.' Her voice was loud in order to penetrate the covering over his ears.

Megan was surprised that Renato obeyed, but she supposed that he didn't have much choice. His arms were still tied behind his back, his eyes and ears covered by the blindfold, and until Leonora chose to release him from his bondage he'd probably worked out that it was better to go along with her demands. In any case, this could hardly be the first time that such a scene had been played out between them. Clearly, behind the bedroom door this was the way they both found satisfaction.

'Here,' Leonora said to Megan, 'use this on him.' She handed Megan an enormous vibrator, the shaft of which was covered in tiny bumps. 'You put it where I had the riding crop handle,' she explained, as Megan looked at it in bewilderment. 'It'll stimulate his prostate and he won't be able to help getting hard again. He may not be able to come, but that doesn't worry me.'

'Please don't, Leonora,' groaned Renato. 'You've no idea how much it hurts when you do this.'

'If it didn't hurt you wouldn't enjoy it. Here, Megan, I've positioned him for you. See how you get on.'

Megan took the vibrator from the other girl, but her fingers were trembling and as she started to insert it between Renato's buttocks he jerked his hips, moving himself away from her. 'Here,' said Leonora, 'use my whip.'

Now it was Megan's turn to stand over Renato, riding crop in one hand and vibrator in the other. All at once her nerves vanished because as she looked down at the tethered man she experienced a sudden surge of power, and understood for the first time why it was such an aphrodisiac.

'You probably won't want him screaming, so cover the head of the vibrator with this,' said Leonora, handing Megan some lubricating jelly. Megan did as the blonde girl suggested and then, when Renato refused to position himself as she wanted him, she raised her arm and for the first time in her life struck another human being's flesh with the deliberate intent of causing discomfort.

Renato uttered a yelp and Megan watched the thin red line appearing on his skin. She remembered how it had felt when she'd been struck by Fabrizio, how the hot burning had turned into a golden streak of pleasure and she knew that it must be the same for Renato. Even if it wasn't, she was past caring, because he was a prisoner at her feet and she could do what she liked with him.

Inserting the vibrator inside him wasn't as easy as she'd expected. He moaned and groaned as she twisted it around, trying to force it past the tight sphincter muscles, but finally it was in. She switched it on and he drew in his breath sharply as it stimulated his most sensitive spot.

'Well done!' cried Leonora, reaching beneath her lover's bent body. 'He's getting harder already. Increase the speed a little.'

'No, don't,' Renato begged Megan.

She hesitated and Leonora looked at her in surprise. 'What's the matter? You're doing really well. Don't spoil it now.'

Megan was as pleased by Leonora's praise as by Renato's response, and ignoring his continuing cries for mercy she did as Leonora suggested.

'There,' cooed the blonde girl, her fingers moving beneath Renato. 'You're lovely and hard now, darling, aren't you?'

'But it hurts,' he groaned.

'You adore it, just as you adore me,' whispered Leonora. 'See if you can come again for me.'

For some time Megan continued to move the vibrator around deep inside Renato's tight back passage, and although he whimpered and groaned he didn't try to move away from her again. Finally, as she flicked intermittently at his back with the riding crop and the vibrator worked remorselessly inside him, Leonora's wicked little fingers brought about a violent shuddering and Renato's initial cry of pain changed to a low guttural sound of animal pleasure.

'Turn it off now,' said Leonora quickly. 'I don't want to really hurt him.'

Briefly Megan hesitated, reluctant to relinquish her power, but then Fabrizio crossed the bedroom floor and turned the vibrator off, removing it from Renato before leading Megan away. 'It seems you enjoyed that more than you expected,' he remarked.

'Yes,' confessed Megan, 'but I feel so ashamed.'

'Why?'

'Because I don't think I'm normal.'

Fabrizio laughed. 'If you were normal you wouldn't be staying here with us. Normal is boring. Here we know how to live life to the full. There's nothing wrong with any of this. You got pleasure from what happened and so did Renato.'

'But some of the time he was in a lot of pain,' Megan pointed out.

'And his pain gave you pleasure, did it not?'

'It shouldn't have done,' muttered Megan.

'In the end you both had pleasure, so where's the harm in it all?' asked Alessandra lightly. 'Come on, we'd better leave these two love-birds alone together.'

Outside the bedroom door Megan paused, unsure as to what she should do next. 'You can go back to bed,' said Fabrizio. 'Come, Alessandra. It's time you and I enjoyed ourselves now.'

Alessandra shot a brief look of triumph at Megan that she tried to conceal behind a smile. 'I'm so glad you were able to join in, Megan,' she said sweetly. 'Your appetite for these things surprises me.'

'It doesn't surprise me,' said Fabrizio, and the smile that he gave Megan was an approving one. 'I always knew she was capable of great things.'

'Goodnight then,' said Megan, wishing that she was the one who had the right to go with Fabrizio to the master bedroom, instead of having to climb the stairs to what she supposed could almost be considered the servants' quarters. Just the same, she felt that she'd done well tonight, and she'd experienced incredible new sensations. She wasn't certain that Renato had enjoyed it as much as the others seemed to think, and she wondered if he was quite as content with Leonora as he appeared to be in the daylight hours.

The next morning Fabrizio received an urgent call from Italy and by midday he'd left the house and was on his way to Tuscany. Alessandra offered to go with him but he made it clear that he wished to travel alone. 'It's a business crisis,' he explained. 'I'll have no time for pleasure.'

'How long will you be gone?'

'A week perhaps, no more.'

'A week!'

Fabrizio smiled. 'If you get desperate you can always join Leonora and Renato. It won't be the first time.'

'I was wondering what we were to do about Megan while you were gone?'

Fabrizio frowned. 'That is a problem. It's a pity, but

for a few days she will have to concentrate her energies on the library. No one's to touch her until I return. Is that clearly understood?'

Alessandra nodded. She'd never question any decision of Fabrizio's but she did wonder why it was that Megan couldn't even join the rest of the household in some form of sexual activity without Fabrizio being present.

When she told the English girl that Fabrizio had gone, Alessandra couldn't help but take pleasure from the look of desolation that crossed Megan's face. 'Why has he gone back to Italy?' she asked.

'It's a crisis, something to do with the family business. He said that you should have plenty to keep you busy while he's gone,' she added.

Megan flushed. 'Yes of course. As a matter of fact, I'm getting on far better than I expected. I think that I'll be finished before the six months are up.'

'Really? It seems you're a quick worker.' Alessandra couldn't keep the note of irony out of her voice, and she knew that Megan understood what she meant because the other girl hastily left the room to start work.

Normally when she was away from Fabrizio,

Alessandra was perfectly content with her own company. He'd been quite right when he'd said that on previous occasions she'd joined Leonora and Renato when she'd wanted sex, but this time that wasn't something that interested her. She was far too busy worrying about whether or not Fabrizio was genuinely obsessed with Megan as a person, or whether it was the experiment alone that was intriguing him.

Grateful that the English summer was far exceeding her expectations, she decided to spend the afternoon in the garden. As usual she was careful to sit in the shade. She couldn't afford for her skin to age prematurely, and although she was naturally olive skinned she never allowed herself a suntan. At twenty-seven she was aware that she was reaching the end of her modelling career and in recent months had begun to hope that she and Fabrizio would become a permanent item. Then she could quit modelling to be his hostess and partner, although she knew that marriage was out of the question. Fabrizio was not the marrying kind. Fortunately, neither was she. All the same, she didn't want the English girl to upset her plans.

She tried to concentrate on a novel that she'd picked up at the airport on her way back from Milan, but although it was an easy read the words made no sense. She was grateful when Renato arrived and provided a welcome diversion.

'I've been looking all over the house for you,' he remarked. 'Isn't it a glorious day?'

'The weather's nice, certainly.'

Renato looked questioningly at her. 'Do I take it that something's bothering you?'

Alessandra trusted Renato. She'd always liked him, and he was far easier to talk to than Fabrizio. 'It's Megan,' she confessed.

He nodded. 'I thought it might be.'

'I think Fabrizio's becoming fond of her. I don't know what I can do about it.'

'There's nothing you can do. I'm not certain that you're right though. She intrigues him, and he's anxious to win his wager with me, which is why he's so delighted that she's taking to everything so enthusiastically. It's a matter of pride and sexual excitement rather than affection. You know him better than I do; is he even capable of affection?'

'No, but he does become obsessed with certain women to the exclusion of all others.'

'He's been obsessed with you for some time,'

admitted Renato. 'I can't believe that Megan Stewart offers serious competition. She's a novelty, that's all.'

Alessandra looked closely at Renato. 'I don't think you really believe that. You're only saying it to make me feel better.'

Renato sighed. 'No, I'm saying it because I hope it's the truth. I know how much the relationship means to you and I'm not entirely comfortable with what's happening to Megan either. I never thought she'd be willing to suffer so much humiliation.'

'You were the one who was humiliated last night,' Alessandra pointed out, but then she wished she hadn't as Renato turned his head away to gaze out over the garden, his eyes avoiding hers. 'I'm sorry, I didn't mean it like that.'

'You're quite right,' he said after a pause. 'I was humiliated and this time it didn't turn me on in the way it usually does. I was aroused physically of course, Leonora's clever enough to know how to do that. The problem is, it didn't feel the same. I was more turned on when it was Megan who was striking me than when it was Leonora.'

'Why on earth was that?' asked Alessandra in surprise.

'I'm not sure. It might be because although she was doing everything that she was told, she did it differently from Leonora. There was a gentleness to her which Leonora lacks. Perhaps I'm becoming tired of Leonora's increasing demands.'

'Have they really increased so much?' asked Alessandra. 'Or is it that you're changing?'

'A little of both perhaps. In a sexual situation like ours, things are bound to progress and perhaps I don't wish to go any further than we've already gone. I like more variation than Leonora does.'

'Did you feel like this before Megan joined us?'

Renato thought for a moment. 'No, I can't say that I did. But then, I hadn't really thought about it. Having such an innocent join us has made me re-assess everything. I'm surprised at how much she turns me on. She couldn't be more different from Leonora and yet—'

'Perhaps that's why,' interrupted Alessandra.

'Perhaps it is,' agreed Renato. 'Perhaps my affair with Leonora has run its course. Maybe I need a change.'

'Do you want Megan?'

Renato shook his head. 'No, not Megan herself. I prefer Italian women. I don't really know what I want,

I only know that for the first time since I met Leonora I'm not fully content.'

'How strange,' murmured Alessandra. 'It seems that Megan's had quite an effect on us all, because that's exactly how I feel too.'

The pair of them exchanged a brief glance and Renato's eyes widened a little. Alessandra knew that for the first time he was looking at her in a different way, a sexual way, and a way that didn't involve Fabrizio. 'I must go and find Leonora,' he said hastily, and as she watched him go Alessandra knew that there was no point in pretending any more. Relationships within the household were no longer the same. The question was, would things return to how they had been once Megan had left?

Chapter Eleven

Leonora wasn't at all happy. In fact, she realised that the times when she was happy were fewer and fewer these days, and it was Renato's fault; he was different now. Only this morning she'd woken to find him with his head between her thighs, his tongue moving knowingly over her throbbing clitoris. Although he'd brought her to orgasm several times and she'd enjoyed the hot, sweet floods of release, she'd also resented the fact that he'd taken her by surprise, forcing her to relinquish control. Afterwards, she'd made her displeasure clear but Renato had shrugged, commenting that she'd seemed to be having a good time and he didn't know why she was complaining. If that was true and he really didn't understand, then they were no longer on the same wavelength.

When she and Renato had first got together Leonora had believed that at last she'd found a man who was the perfect partner for her. It no longer looked that way, however, and she was still trying to work out where it had gone wrong.

'Good morning, Leonora,' called Franco, as he crossed the lawn. 'You're not looking very cheerful.'

'What's that to you?' she snapped.

'I can't help noticing that you've lost a lot of your zest for life recently, which upsets me.'

'Why should it upset you?'

'Because I enjoy life and I enjoy women who enjoy it. It's as I told you, Renato doesn't know how to look after you.'

'How do you know it's got anything to do with Renato?'

'Unless one of your horses has gone lame it has to be sex that's making you miserable, and sex and Renato are inseparable where you're concerned.'

'You think you're clever don't you?'

'I observe what's going on in the house and I make

my own deductions. If you weren't so self-obsessed you'd understand what was really happening.'

'What do you mean?'

'That our little librarian's spoiling things for everyone.'

'Everyone?'

'Alessandra's hardly the carefree, smiling girl she used to be. She's afraid that Megan's stealing your brother's heart. You're afraid that Renato's attracted to Megan. That doesn't leave very many happy people here does it? Apart from your brother of course.'

'You look pretty pleased with yourself.'

'Megan's presence here hasn't affected me.'

'It hasn't affected me either,' said Leonora firmly.

'Do you really believe that?'

She sighed, and then her shoulders slumped. 'I don't know. Perhaps you're right, maybe I just don't want to believe it. Why would a natural submissive like Renato be affected by Megan?'

'I thought Megan played the dominant role quite well last night.'

Leonora's eyes flashed. 'How do you know that?'

'I have my ways of finding out what's going on, even

when I'm excluded from your sessions. Well, was she good or wasn't she?'

'She was all right. That's not why he likes her though. I can tell that he likes her softness, her femininity. Personally I think she's wet.'

'I don't think she's as wet as you imagine. She's very clever. It isn't easy to enter a whole new world like she has without panicking at some stage. She's either a very good actress or a genuinely sensual young woman who's fallen for Fabrizio, and who's lucky enough to interest him.'

'Surely not to the exclusion of Alessandra?'

'I think Alessandra suspects that's the case.'

'We were all so happy before she came,' complained Leonora. 'I don't understand why Fabrizio wanted her here.'

'Because he, like you, is easily bored. If he had to be in England for several months he needed a sexual diversion, and perhaps he guessed that you'd all be affected. You know how much your brother likes games of any kind, psychological ones as well as sexual.'

They were back at the house now, and abruptly Franco's hands grabbed Leonora's shoulders and he pinned her against the wall beside the front door, pressing his body up against her before placing his lips on the soft flesh of her neck and sucking hard. When he removed his mouth there was a tiny red mark on her skin, a mark that for a fleeting moment made her his.

'How dare you!' shouted Leonora, and twisting her body she pushed him away from her, her left knee catching him in the groin so that he doubled up with pain and staggered away.

'You bitch,' he groaned.

'You should have known better after our first encounter. It's easy to put you out of action. Call your-self a man?'

Franco's blue eyes glittered with a mixture of rage and excitement. 'Yes, I do call myself a man. I could satisfy you far better than Renato, but you're afraid to let me.'

'I'm not turned on by your macho displays of force.'

Slowly Franco managed to straighten himself, then he lunged back towards Leonora, his hand sliding beneath her skirt until his fingers were between her thighs. 'You can lie with your mouth but your body betrays you,' he laughed, as his fingers moved over the damp material. 'If this can make you wet, just imagine what would happen if you let me do what I want to.'

'You'd never let *me* do what I want to,' Leonora pointed out acidly.

'We'd be equals, you and I. You could fight me, but you might not always win. With Renato there's no contest, that's why you're becoming bored.'

For the first time Leonora looked confused. 'I don't know what I want any more,' she confessed. 'I wish that stupid girl had never come here.'

'With Fabrizio away you could have some fun with her,' Franco suggested slyly.

Leonora's face brightened. 'I hadn't thought of that. Not that my brother would be very pleased, but there's nothing he can do about it. He didn't tell me to leave her alone.'

'He did tell Alessandra that she should be left alone.'

'You know everything don't you?' There was a note of admiration in Leonora's voice.

'Not everything, but most things. What do you think?'

'Did you have anything special in mind?'

'I wondered if we could get her into the cellar. She's never been there, and it would come as quite a shock to her. Also, no one would be able to hear her if she made a fuss.'

Leonora looked doubtful. 'We'd have to be careful. We mustn't hurt her or Fabrizio would go mad.'

'I'm not talking about hurting her, just punishing her a little. There are lots of ways we can do that.'

'We'd never get her to the cellar. She and I aren't particularly good friends. She wouldn't be silly enough to agree to go.'

'She might, if you told her that Fabrizio had phoned and said that he'd remembered there were some books down there. She's very anxious to organise the library perfectly.'

At last Leonora began to feel happy again. 'Now that's what I call a good idea,' she said admiringly. 'When shall I fetch her?'

'After lunch, that's when the others usually have their siesta. Megan always keeps working.'

'And what exactly are we going to do to her?'

'I'll have to think about it.'

'Remember, we have to be careful,' Leonora reminded him.

'Don't worry so much. You can trust me.'

'Yes,' said Leonora slowly. 'I'm beginning to think that I can.'

*

Megan was the last to leave the dining room after lunch, and as she turned left to return to the library she bumped into Leonora.

'Sorry!' said the blonde girl, and Megan was struck once again by how beautiful Fabrizio's sister was. The combination of her jet black eyes, so like her brother's, and her honey-blonde hair was amazing. Megan wished that she liked Leonora more, but there was something about the girl that she couldn't take to. She suspected that the antipathy was mutual.

'I didn't realise you were there,' said Megan.

'It was my fault. I'd forgotten to say at lunch that Fabrizio rang this morning. He meant to tell you before he left that there are some books in the cellar that he'd forgotten to mention. I suppose they're an overspill from the library. Apparently my uncle left them there and Fabrizio thought you ought to have a look at them to make sure they don't need any restoration work before you put them on the shelves.'

'I hope they've been well packaged,' said Megan, horrified at the thought of the damage that could have occurred in a damp cellar.

'Do you know where the cellar is?' asked Leonora casually.

Megan shook her head. 'I didn't even know there was one.'

'It's near the stables, but you can get to it through a short underground passage from the back of the walk-in larder. Come on, I'll show you.'

Megan followed Leonora through the kitchen and into the large, cool pantry. At the far end a metal ring was set into one of the floor slabs and as Leonora pulled it up Megan saw a small metal ladder going down to a floor beneath the house. 'This is fun,' she said excitedly. 'Like smuggling or something.'

'What's smuggling?' asked Leonora.

'I don't know the Italian for it,' apologised Megan. 'It's contraband, you know, when people used to bring alcohol into the country in barrels and keep it hidden away for special clients.'

'Ah, smugglers, yes. Like the ones in *Carmen*. I adore Carmen. She was so passionate, but also cruel,' said Leonora. Megan was surprised at how excited the other girl looked.

Just as she was about to descend the ladder, Megan hesitated. She didn't know why but the hairs on the back of her neck were prickling with fear.

'What's the matter?' asked Leonora. 'You're not

afraid of slipping are you? I'll go first. It's very easy.'
Megan stood back and then, reluctantly, followed
Leonora down into the darkness of the secret passage-
way. 'Imagine, we're walking under the garden,'
laughed Leonora. 'It's not a very convenient place to
have a cellar. Rather a long way for the servants to go
every time the master of the house wanted a fresh
bottle of wine.'

'Is it where Fabrizio keeps his wine?'

Leonora shook her head. 'No, my uncle had a special
wine cellar built in the main body of the house with the
air temperature controlled. Some of the wine's incredibly valuable.'

'I can't imagine why your uncle had his books taken
all this way,' said Megan as they approached the door
to the cellar. 'It would have been far simpler if he'd
stacked them in the attic.'

'It does seem odd,' conceded Leonora. 'Still, as he's
dead we can't really ask him why he did it, can we?'

There was no excitement in this for Megan now. She
didn't like the feeling of being underground, nor did she
fancy rummaging around in a cold, dank, disused
cellar, disturbing loads of spiders and, horror of hor-
rors, possibly rats, as she trailed back and forth with

packages of books. 'Do you know how many books there are down here?'

'No idea,' said Leonora casually. 'Never mind, we'll find out now,' and she pushed on the heavy cellar door.

To Megan's surprise the door didn't creak as it opened; the hinges were well oiled and she wondered why. Leonora stepped in first. 'Come on, I'll put the light on but I'll have to shut the door first or I can't get at the switch.'

Megan took three tentative steps into the darkness, peering into the gloom, and then jumped as the door slammed shut behind her and she heard a bolt thrust home. 'What are you doing?' she cried, then the light was switched on and she saw Franco standing in the middle of the room.

'You got her here,' he said softly to Leonora. Whirling around Megan tried frantically to open the cellar door, but her hands couldn't manage the heavy bolt in time and Franco's arms went around her waist and pulled her away. She kicked out violently as he carried her across the floor of the cellar before throwing her face down on a hard, narrow bed at the far end of the room.

'This is one of Fabrizio's little playrooms,' he told

her. 'No doubt he would have shown it to you himself in time, but Leonora and I decided that we'd like to be the ones to introduce you to some of his more esoteric tastes. Have you got everything ready, Leonora?'

'Yes.'

Megan's heart was thumping violently against her ribcage, and as Franco pulled her up off the bed and manhandled her into the middle of the room she glanced around her. There was a large beam suspended from the ceiling and attached to it was a heavy metal ring with a rope through it. On the end of the rope were handcuffs. When she realised that Franco and Leonora intended to use the cuffs on her she began to fight even harder, but it was useless. Franco was muscular and strong. Within seconds he'd imprisoned her hands above her head, forcing her on to tiptoes, and then the cuffs were clipped into place and she was suspended, her arms stretched tightly above her and the muscles in her legs aching because of the position she was in.

'She'd look better naked,' said Leonora thoughtfully.

'We needed to get her secured first,' explained Franco. 'You're quite a little fighter aren't you?' he added, and his fingers pinched Megan's left breast through her blouse. She gave a squeal, then Franco hooked two fingers in to the 'v' of her blouse and pulled violently downwards, tearing the fabric. She heard the buttons falling to the floor. Leonora parted the tattered cotton, pulling it back and tying the ends behind Megan's back, which only left her bra covering her breasts. Unfortunately for her this was a front fastening bra and soon her top half was totally exposed.

She was wearing a button-through skirt which made it easy for Franco to remove it, and then she was hanging suspended from the beam, the cool air of the cellar touching her bare flesh, and she wondered how long it would be before her white cotton panties were removed as well, completing her humiliation.

'There's no need to look so frightened,' said Leonora, running the backs of her fingers across Megan's belly. Megan's muscles jerked instinctively and Leonora laughed softly, allowing her fingers to trail on upwards, lightly brushing the undersides of each of Megan's breasts. 'We're not going to hurt you; Fabrizio wouldn't like that.'

'Then why have you brought me here?' demanded Megan.

'For some fun.'

'I want to leave,' said Megan firmly.

'And so you will, but not until we've finished with you,' said Franco. 'Let me see, I think we'll start with the feathers, Leonora.'

'That's a good idea,' agreed Leonora excitedly. 'You'll enjoy this, Megan.'

The Italian girl crossed the room and Megan could hear her moving about behind her.

'There's everything here that we need,' explained Franco, his cold blue eyes fixed on the chained girl. 'You have to admire Fabrizio, he thinks of every eventuality.' Leonora returned carrying two large ostrich feathers. She handed one to Franco, who moved behind Megan and then, working in unison, the pair of them started to caress the tightly stretched body with the plumes.

Franco worked upwards from the calves of her legs, using long sweeping motions. It felt delicious, especially combined with what Leonora was doing. She was using her plume on Megan's breasts, sweeping it from side to side and allowing the tip to tickle Megan's armpits. Then, as Megan started to squirm, she moved the plume around each breast in turn, the circular movements causing the girl's breasts to harden and the nipples to become painfully rigid as she grew more and more excited.

Franco's feather was still working on the backs of her legs and thighs and once or twice her toes lost contact with the ground as her muscles spasmed in pleasurable response to what he was doing. Each time this happened pain would rush through her arms, which were then forced to take the full weight of her body, and she'd scrabble frantically to get her feet back on the floor. Soon it became a constant fight to subdue her excited flesh in order to prevent the pain that came with each muscular spasm of pleasure. 'You're enjoying this, aren't you?' asked Leonora. There was genuine curiosity in her voice.

Megan didn't answer. Her body was enjoying the physical sensations that they were arousing in her, but she didn't like being chained as she was. Neither did she like the fact that the pair of them had her in a cellar a long way from the house, and that no one knew she was there except for them. She was well aware that whatever they did, however loud she shouted, no one would hear her. She was completely at their mercy.

'She isn't going to admit it,' laughed Franco. 'We'll have to see if we can increase the pleasure. It's time we got those schoolgirl knickers off her. I'm sure she'd like a little stimulation between her thighs.'

Megan kept very still as Franco hooked the fingers of both hands into the sides of her panties before tugging them down, and then she was ordered to lift both her feet at once. She refused, knowing how much this would hurt her arms. At first it seemed that her refusal was accepted because Leonora seemed indifferent and Franco moved away. Suddenly she felt a stinging blow round her waist and the tip of a whip dug into her flesh. 'I'm very good at this,' said Franco, his voice thick with excitement. 'Although normally I use much more strength. Now, will you do as we tell you or not?'

As Megan gasped with the shock of the receding pain she decided to obey, and gritted her teeth as she bent her knees, lifting her feet off the ground to allow them to remove her panties. Then, as her feet once more took the weight off her aching shoulders, she waited to see how they were going to arouse her next.

Franco and Leonora stood in front of the suspended Megan and looked thoughtfully at her, before glancing at each other with knowing smiles. Just the fact that they were looking at her made Megan's nipples harden. Franco stepped foward and slowly ran his hands around her hips while his tongue moved lazily over her belly. Her excitement grew and she started to feel hot with desire.

'She's loving this,' he said softly.

'But she's still afraid,' responded Leonora. 'I can see it in her eyes.'

It was true. The things that they were doing to her were slowly driving Megan wild, but she was still acutely aware of how helpless she was, knowing that if they wanted to they could inflict just as much pain as pleasure.

Leaning down, Franco pushed Megan's legs apart and she uttered a tiny moan of protest as her arms once more took the full weight of her body. 'If you don't like it I'll stop,' he said.

'No, I don't want you to stop,' confessed Megan, then shuddered as his mouth moved along the creases at the tops of her thighs, planting tiny kisses on the tender flesh. She could feel her clitoris hardening and there was an aching deep inside her as her vagina swelled in anticipation of being filled. Her climax was getting nearer now and when Franco abruptly inserted two fingers inside her she moaned with delight. Then, for a few delicious, tantalising seconds he rubbed the side of her clitoris until she felt her muscles tighten. Her body arched as she teetered on the edge of a climax.

Roughly Franco withdrew his fingers and, stepping back, he studied Megan again. She stared at him. She could imagine only too well how she must look and tried to keep her eyes expressionless, but she guessed that her need must show because both her tormentors looked very pleased with themselves. She guessed that this was how they were going to make her suffer; by arousing and re-arousing her, and enjoying her humiliation as she remained their prisoner, unable either to suppress her excitement or to have her pleasure spill, unless they chose to allow it. Somehow she didn't imagine that was going to happen.

For a few minutes they left her alone, and although the tension in her body subsided a little, her need for a climax didn't. Now Leonora began to caress her nipples with the feathered plume again and the sweet aching was so exquisite that Megan gave a cry of delight. 'That's good, isn't it?' murmured Leonora. 'I know how it feels, it's so good that you can't wait for the pleasure to increase.' As she was talking she allowed the plume to swirl down over Megan's stomach, then dipped the tip into her belly button until Megan began to squirm, almost out of her mind with need as her burgeoning flesh screamed for satisfaction.

'Put that down and come and help me,' Franco commanded Leonora, and with a regretful sigh Fabrizio's sister obeyed. Now she too began to work between Megan's legs. On Franco's orders she parted Megan's sex lips so that Franco could examine their prisoner better. Trailing a finger in the moisture that was seeping from Megan's entrance he laughed. 'Shall I spread some of this around your tight little clit,' he murmured and, hoping that this would allow her to come, Megan nodded. 'Beg me,' said Franco.

Megan was past caring about pride, all she wanted was to feel the delicious release that her body needed so urgently. 'Please, please do,' she begged.

'Doesn't she sound sweet,' said Leonora.

'Very sweet,' agreed Franco, and his fingers moved in a gentle circle around her frantic clitoris then, as she felt the hot pulsations begin, his fingers tightened cruelly around the delicate bud and pain streaked up from her clitoris, through the engorged pelvic muscles and her lower belly and she uttered a cry of pain.

'You're not meant to hurt her,' said Leonora angrily.

'I had to, she was about to come,' said Franco casually. 'I hadn't realised how near she was.'

Megan was weeping now, not because of the pain but because she was tired of being toyed with. Every muscle in her body was so tense and tight that she didn't know what to do. She wished that she could control herself better, that she could stop them from arousing her, but they were too skilful. As soon as the pain died away and her body was still once more, they resumed their attentions. Franco's fingers plunged repeatedly in and out of her, continuing to titillate the moist inner channel but without touching her clitoris. Leonora spread some of Megan's juices around to the back of her and, inserting the tip of her little finger into Megan's rectum, pressed against the sides until Megan's muscles started to slither and coil as the dark pleasure began.

For nearly half an hour they played with her, keeping her teetering on the brink of release but never allowing her even the smallest orgasm until she felt ready to explode. She was sobbing constantly, begging them to let her come, but the more she begged the more they laughed until eventually she forced herself to keep silent.

'Time to put her on the bed I think,' said Franco. 'Are you ready to move on to stage two, Leonora?'

Megan saw Leonora nod in agreement and she trembled with fear, wondering what stage two would involve. Swiftly, Franco's strong arms unfastened her and she gave an involuntary sigh of relief as she was at last able to let her arms hang by her sides. Her relief was short-lived, however, because the pair of them lay her on the bed and then tightened straps around her, one over her hips, the other just beneath her breasts, at the same time leaving her arms free.

Once they were certain that she couldn't escape, Leonora and Franco stripped off their clothes, and Megan could see that both of them were highly aroused. Clearly, turning her on had been an aphrodisiac for them. Leonora's breasts were full and tight, and she had the pink flush of arousal over her neck and chest. As for Franco, his erection was rock hard, the tip of the glans purple and the veins standing out.

Leonora bent over the fastened Megan and lightly touched her breasts. 'It's our turn now,' she said sweetly. 'We don't want you to feel left out though, so we're going to let you join in, but only a little.'

'Are you going to let me come?' whispered Megan.

Leonora's dark eyes danced with amusement. 'Of course not, silly! We're going to let you help us gain our pleasure, that's all.'

'I don't see why I should,' said Megan. 'Your brother's not going to like it when he hears about this,' she added.

'I wouldn't tell him if I were you,' said Leonora. 'If you do we might bring you back here and really hurt you. Even if it made Fabrizio angry that wouldn't help you. Somehow I don't think you'd enjoy it one little bit, do you?'

'It isn't fair,' wailed Megan. 'Why are you doing this to me?'

'Because I wish you'd never come to our house,' said Leonora.

'Why?' asked Megan, totally bewildered.

'Because you've changed things.'

'In what way?'

'There's no need to tell her anything else,' interrupted Franco. 'Come on, let's get on with this.'

Leonora climbed quickly onto the bed, crouching on all fours above the chained girl. Then she bent her arms so that her upper body was lowered, angling herself to make sure that her breasts were within reach of Megan's lips. 'Start sucking on my nipples,' she commanded her.

'You can begin with whichever one you like, they're equally sensitive, like yours I expect,' and she brushed the palm of her hand idly over Megan's aching nipples.

'Please don't touch me again,' Megan begged her.

'You shouldn't plead with us like that,' said Leonora. 'It's a mistake. You see, neither of us have a better nature to which you can appeal. You simply make us want to torment you all the more.'

'But I need to come,' cried Megan.

'I'm sure Fabrizio will oblige you once he gets home. Now, do as I say.' Leonora pushed her left breast on to Megan's mouth. Realising that she had no choice, Megan began to suck lightly on the other girl's nipple.

'Harder than that,' said Leonora, 'and use your lips *and* teeth. I like to feel teeth grazing my nipples. You can bite a little if you want.'

Obediently, Megan started to suck harder, and as Leonora uttered a sigh of contentment Megan felt her own excitement increasing. She liked the sensation of her tongue moving over Leonora's tanned, smooth skin, and as her teeth nipped obediently at the rigid little bud she felt her own nipples harden and tingle in pleasurable response.

'How's she doing?' asked Franco.

'Very well.'

'Good,' murmured Franco, as he too climbed onto the bed. Kneeling behind Leonora he rested his hands on the sides of the bed, his fingers splayed out so that his thumbs were just touching Megan's waist, and he thrust himself inside Leonora. The force of his action pushed the blonde-haired girl's body down even lower, so that Megan had to open her mouth wider and draw in more of the girl's breast. She could hear Leonora groaning with delight, and every time Franco moved powerfully in and out of his lover, Megan felt the vibrations through Leonora's body.

It was an extraordinary experience, but as she moved her mouth from one breast to the other, hearing Leonora's loud, guttural cries of rising passion, Megan's own body swelled, until the straps that were holding her to the bed cut painfully into her damp, aroused flesh. The ache between her thighs was sharp, like a painful throbbing void, and closing her eyes she tried to imagine what it would be like if Franco was thrusting into her rather than into the girl crouched above her.

His rhythm was faster now, but still smooth, and Megan could tell that he was approaching his own climax. Suddenly, without thinking about what she was doing, she reached up with one of her free hands and lightly tickled Leonora's gently rounded belly. At the same time her teeth fastened tightly around the base of the crouching girl's nipple and with a startled scream of pleasure Leonora climaxed.

Megan continued to suck and lick on Leonora's imprisoned breast and her fingers kept moving over the other girl's belly so that she could feel the rhythmic contractions of her climax, a climax that Megan longed to share and which her thwarted body so desperately needed. A few seconds later Franco threw back his head and cried out in Italian as his whole body was shaken and he flooded Leonora with his hot seed.

When it was over Leonora and Franco fell forward and for a short time Megan had to take the weight of both of them. Frantic for relief she tried to thrust her hips upwards, to stimulate her pubic bone against the heavy weight of the satisfied couple, but just as the first delicious tingles began inside her the other two realised what she was doing and, pulling themselves upright, they scrambled off the bed. 'Naughty!' said Leonora reprovingly.

'Can't I come now?' begged Megan, ashamed to hear herself uttering the words but unable to suppress them.

'Sorry, maybe another time. That was fantastic, Franco. You were right, this was a good idea of yours. I feel much better now.'

'I don't think our little English librarian does,' laughed Franco, and bending over the bed he allowed his tongue to stray between Megan's sex lips for a few final seconds, pressing the tip just inside her and then withdrawing it as her muscles gave an involuntary jerk of pleasure.

'We'll get dressed, then unfasten you and leave. You can dress yourself and follow when you feel like it,' he said casually.

'We'll leave you a little present when we go,' promised Leonora.

A few minutes later the pair of them were dressed, and as Franco unfastened Megan, Leonora bent down, placing something on the floor beside the bed. Then, as Megan heard a clicking sound, the pair of them left. While Megan dressed, the tiny tape recorder that Leonora had brought with her at the start of the afternoon played back all that had happened, and Megan listened to her own frantic cries, her mounting excitement and desperate begging for relief.

She could have turned it off at any time and couldn't

understand why she didn't, but there was a dreadful fascination about it all. She knew that despite everything she'd endured, what had happened to her this afternoon had given her pleasure, albeit of a new kind.

She wanted to masturbate now that the other two had gone, to give herself the relief that she so urgently needed, but, afraid that there might be a concealed camera somewhere in the room, she didn't give in to the craving. Instead, after she'd dressed and heard the tape through to the end, she left the cellar and made her way back to the house.

It was only once she'd reached the safety of her own room, run herself a hot bath and was lying in the warm scented water that she at last allowed her fingers to roam between her thighs. To her shame, the moment her fingertips touched the side of the stem of her clitoris her body was racked by a huge orgasm. It was so intense that despite being on her own she uttered a scream of ecstatic delight because now, after all the hours of thwarted need, her body was finally flooded with the long awaited pleasure and she was at last able to relax.

As she lay there, bringing herself to a more leisurely second orgasm, she realised how much she'd changed since joining the Balocchi household.

Chapter Twelve

It was two weeks before Fabrizio returned to Sussex. After her session in the cellar with Leonora and Franco, Megan had been left alone. With nothing to do but work she'd virtually finished organising the library by the time he finally came back.

Watching him walk to the front door, briefcase in hand, she started to tremble with excitement, and to her delight he came straight to her.

'How's it going?' he asked, his eyes flicking round the room.

'I'll be finished tomorrow.'

Fabrizio looked stunned. 'So soon?'

'I've had few distractions with you away.'

He thought for a moment. 'Tonight I shall distract you once more. Come to my bedroom at midnight, but tell no one.'

Megan nodded, her body aflame with desire. A whole night alone with him was more than she'd dared hope for, especially so soon after his return, and she wondered how he was going to get rid of Alessandra.

Alessandra had just finished undressing and was about to join Fabrizio on their bed when there was a light tap on the door. 'Who can that be?' she asked.

Fabrizio smiled. 'It's Megan. I invited her, but she isn't expecting to find you here also.' Before Alessandra could protest he called for Megan to enter, and the two women looked at each other with a mixture of surprise and hostility.

Megan hesitated in the doorway. 'I thought ...'

'That we'd be alone?' asked Fabrizio. Megan nodded. 'So did Alessandra, but I've missed you both while I've been away. Now we can make up for lost time. Close the door, Megan, then we can begin.' He saw the doubt and confusion in her eyes, and heard Alessandra's hiss of displeasure, but Megan obeyed and, propping himself up on the bed, he smiled at them both.

'I want you to enjoy yourselves, to get to know each other as intimately as possible by both giving and receiving pleasure. Eventually I shall join in, but I wish you to begin without me. Alessandra, as the more experienced, I suggest you start the night off for us all.'

It seemed that Alessandra was going to refuse at first, but then, clearly realising that there was a great deal at stake, she walked across the room and began to undress Megan. Megan felt the other girl's hands unfastening the silk wrap-around robe that she'd put on especially for Fabrizio. Then, as it slid to the floor with a soft rustling sound, Alessandra slipped the straps of the matching ankle-length nightdress down over Megan's shoulders until her arms were imprisoned at her sides. Finally, she bent her head and started to use her tongue on the girl's exposed breasts.

The touch was incredibly delicate, the tip of her tongue so light that at times Megan could scarcely bear it. She felt as though she needed more pressure, yet at the same time it felt delicious and she began to wriggle with rising excitement. Alessandra touched Megan on the cheek and then moved her mouth up over Megan's neck, kissing the skin as she went. It was all wonderfully arousing and soon Alessandra began to concentrate on Megan's ears and earlobes, gently pushing her tongue in and out in an imitation of penetration. The light tickling feeling quickly had Megan moaning with excitement. Again Alessandra started to kiss and nibble on Megan's neck, and Megan lifted her face, revelling in the sensuous pleasure that was enveloping her.

When Alessandra allowed her tongue to trail upwards again, moving in swirls around the earlobe, Megan's whole body tightened as she waited for the delicate point to enter her ear once more. When it finally did, her body shook gently with a tiny orgasm.

Alessandra looked directly into Megan's eyes and smiled at her. 'Did you like that?'

'Oh yes,' moaned Megan.

'I thought you would,' murmured Alessandra. She pulled Megan's nightdress down to the floor so that both women were naked and then, holding out her hand, she led Megan over to the bed, which was now empty as Fabrizio was sitting in an armchair by the window.

The two women lay down and, filled with gratitude for the pleasure she'd just received, Megan started to arouse Alessandra. She buried her face in the tawny-haired girl's breasts, sucking on them, gently at first but then harder until Alessandra began to groan. Encouraged by this, Megan pushed Alessandra's breasts together so that she could get both nipples into her mouth at the same time. As she allowed her teeth to graze against the hard, pointed peaks, Alessandra's body started to contort, her hips twisting frantically on the bed as she rubbed her vulva against Megan's thigh. Megan moved her leg from side to side in a rocking motion which drove Alessandra into a mad frenzy, and only a few seconds later Megan felt the beautiful olive-skinned girl convulse in an ecstasy of passion, swept by an intense orgasm.

As soon as she'd recovered, Alessandra moved on top of Megan, but this time with her head between Megan's aching thighs, her fingers parting the other girl's swollen labia. When her softly caressing tongue finally lapped at Megan's throbbing clitoris, Megan screamed with delight and started to come again, her body shaken by long, shuddering spasms. The spasms went on and on because Alessandra continued to lick and suck at the delicate collection of nerve endings until Megan was so sensitive that she attempted to bring her legs together in order to stop Alessandra.

Taking the hint Alessandra lifted her head. 'Now you can do the same for me,' she gasped, and Megan was delighted to oblige. She knew that her tongue was not as skilful as Alessandra's, nor her touch so knowing, but despite this the Italian girl was soon uttering tiny mewing sounds of pleasure. Megan was vaguely aware that Fabrizio was standing behind her, watching his lover as her eyelids closed over her large violet eyes just before her muscles spasmed violently and her head thrashed from side to side while she screamed with delight.

'I can't wait any longer,' he said hoarsely, and tearing off his clothes he joined the two young women on the bed.

Swiftly he bent over Alessandra, whose eyes were still closed, and Megan watched as he slowly poured oil over the girl's breasts and stomach, rubbing it in with firm circular movements that made her open her eyes. 'It feels so good,' she murmured.

'What I have planned will feel even better,' he

murmured, and proceeded to continue spreading the oil over her hips, belly and legs.

Megan's own body ached with a desire to have him rub the oil into her, but instead he pulled her down on top of his lover so that the women were lying with their breasts touching, and then he started to move Megan's body over Alessandra's. His hands gripped her hips as he manoeuvred her up and down, occasionally pressing her breasts down hard against Alessandra's.

The feeling was incredible and both Megan and Alessandra grew more and more excited as he brought them nearer and nearer to a climax. As he worked, his tongue moved up and down Megan's spine and then, as Alessandra began to climax and Megan's own belly tightened in response to the feel of the muscles rippling beneath her he let his tongue probe between the cheeks of her bottom. He licked the highly sensitive flesh at the base of her spine and at the same time moved a hand beneath her, so that his fingers could move over her vulva, soaked by her own juices. Immediately she climaxed and as her body trembled violently Alessandra's was re-stimulated and the pair of them climaxed together.

Megan thought she'd go out of her mind with excitement. It was all so new and different, but Fabrizio hadn't finished yet. As the two women's bodies writhed on the bed he pulled them nearer the edge and then, bending over, parted the cheeks of Megan's bottom. After pouring a little oil onto himself he thrust deep inside her rectum. She was now used to this dark, forbidden pleasure that was so different from any other, and could have wept with gratitude as he moved carefully in and out of her, arousing the delicate nerve endings to fever-pitch.

As she teetered on the brink of release he gave one final savage thrust that pushed both of them over the edge, and while Megan and Fabrizio cried out in delighted unison, Alessandra lay sated but motionless beneath them. Looking into the other girl's eyes Megan saw that despite all the pleasure she'd received Alessandra was looking sad, and she guessed that the other girl suspected that Fabrizio cared more about giving Megan pleasure than he did about pleasuring her.

If Alessandra needed further proof she quickly received it, because as soon as he'd withdrawn from Megan, Fabrizio pulled her to her feet. He then pushed her into the armchair, hooking her legs over the arms of the chair, which left her totally exposed to him. Still trembling from the aftermath of the violence of her previous orgasm, Megan watched wide-eyed as he approached her with a large vibrator which he then thrust deep inside her vagina, twisting and turning it against her internal walls.

Again the incredible, hot pressure began to build inside her, but as the tingles started to spread through her lower belly he pulled the vibrator out, moving it up and down the slick inner passage between her outer sex lips so that for a brief moment release was denied to her. Then, as she started to whimper with frustration, he moved it back inside her and with his other hand gripped her right breast hard, his fingertips digging deep into the tender flesh. The combination of pain and pleasure produced another shattering orgasm and Megan screamed.

'Oh God, yes! Yes!' she shouted, and when Fabrizio started to kiss her, Alessandra walked naked from the bedroom, closing the door quietly behind her.

'What are you doing up so early?' Renato asked Alessandra as he walked into the kitchen to make himself a coffee at six o'clock the next morning.

'I've ordered a taxi to take me to the airport. I'm going home,' she said shortly.

Renato stared at her. 'But why?'

'Because Fabrizio doesn't need me anymore. He prefers Megan.'

Renato frowned. 'Are you certain?'

She laughed bitterly. 'Believe me, after what I saw last night there's no room for doubt. I don't intend to outstay my welcome. Besides, Megan's tougher than she looks. She won't want me around any longer. I could tell that she realised for the first time what a hold she's got on Fabrizio. Although in this household three isn't necessarily a crowd, it is where Megan and I are concerned.'

'Then I've lost five thousand pounds thanks to her. You might be interested to know that I'm returning home too,' said Renato.

'You? Why's that?'

He shrugged. 'In a way our reasons are similar. Leonora and I have travelled as far as we can together. She's with Franco now, and anyway Fabrizio would like me to run the Balocchi business in Italy. I think he wishes to stay on here.'

'I'm sure he does. He and Megan will probably have a wonderful time in this house.'

'Why don't we go together?' suggested Renato diffidently. 'I've always admired you, you know that. It's just that I'm not at all like Fabrizio and so I wasn't sure ...'

'How I felt about you?'

'Yes.'

'Why don't we give it a try?' she said softly. 'I think perhaps I'd enjoy having a partner who wasn't quite so insistent on control. But are you sure about Leonora and Franco? They don't seem a likely pair.'

'I think they suit each other very well,' said Renato slowly. 'He'll probably expand Leonora's horizons.'

'But won't Fabrizio object? After all, Franco's only his secretary.'

'That's not our worry is it?'

Alessandra smiled. 'No, you're quite right, it isn't. If you're really serious, come away with me now before Fabrizio gets up. It will serve him right to find me gone and his sister partnered with his secretary, don't you think?'

'I think we should concentrate on ourselves,' said Renato. Then he too smiled. 'All the same, I'd like to see his face when he does get up.'

Half an hour later Alessandra and Renato were

speeding in a taxi to the airport, bound for Tuscany and the main office of the Balocchi family empire.

'Where's Alessandra?' demanded Fabrizio later that morning.

Leonora, who was busy talking to Franco, glanced at her brother with a glint of amusement in her eyes. 'She's gone.'

'Gone where?'

'Back to Italy.'

Only the slight tightening of the muscles in his jaw indicated his annoyance. 'When will she be back?'

'I don't think she will,' replied Leonora. 'Here, she left this letter for you. Apparently it explains everything.'

Fabrizio tore open the envelope and his eyes scanned the two beautifully hand-written pages. 'It appears that Renato has also gone.' Leonora nodded. 'Doesn't that upset you?' asked Fabrizio.

'Not really. I'd already decided that Franco suits me better.'

Fabrizio opened his mouth as though to object, but then turned away. 'As you wish. I've got what I want, why should I stand in your way?'

Leonora raised her eyebrows. 'Then you don't mind that Alessandra's left you?'

'She hasn't left me, she was never with me. We simply enjoyed ourselves when we were together.'

'I see. And now you and Megan are going to enjoy yourselves together, is that it?'

Fabrizio nodded. 'Yes, that's it exactly. You should be grateful. If I wasn't so pleased with the way things have worked out, I might be less accepting about your new choice of partner.'

'Franco and I will just have to hope that Megan keeps you happy then,' said Leonora with a laugh.

'I'm sure she will,' he said confidently.

Leonora looked sceptical. 'For a time, yes, no doubt she will, but you know how easily you get bored. Why should Megan be any different from Alessandra? Or Alessandra's predecessors come to that?'

'Nothing lasts for ever,' retorted her brother as he left the room.

'It may not with him,' said Franco as he pulled Leonora hard against him, his right hand reaching inside her dress to roughly pinch her nipples, 'but nothing's going to come between you and me. I've waited too long for you to let that happen.'

'Then you'll have to make sure I don't get bored, won't you?' said Leonora challengingly.

'I don't think that will be a problem,' said Franco, and as his fingers closed around Leonora's nipple she began to whimper with pain and struggled violently. Soon the pair of them were locked in an embrace that was half fight and half uncontrollable lust.

Chapter Thirteen

Four weeks later Megan sat outside in the summer swing-seat of the Sussex garden, rocking gently back and forth. To the casual eye she appeared to be relaxing, gazing dreamily into space and enjoying the beautiful weather. The reality was rather different. In fact her arms were stretched out tightly on either side of her, her wrists fastened with long, thin pieces of rope, and the skirt of her dress had been pushed up and tucked beneath her so that her legs were bare from the middle of her thighs down.

Her face was taut with sexual tension, her eyes wide and desperate and there were tiny beads of perspiration on her top lip. Slowly the swing seat stopped moving and she tried frantically to wriggle her body sufficiently to start it again, because the love-balls that Fabrizio had inserted inside her before putting her outside provided her with delicious stimulation when the seat was in motion. Unfortunately, the stimulation was never quite enough to allow her to climax but after half an hour she knew that she was very near and felt certain that once the seat resumed swinging she'd finally come.

'Time for another push I think,' said Fabrizio, his deep voice calm, as though he had no idea how she was feeling. She watched him as he moved out of her range of vision and then felt his hands pushing the seat, so that once more the wonderful tingling started deep inside her, sending sparks of excitement streaking through her body and she whimpered with pleasure.

'Have you come yet?' he asked with interest.

'No,' she groaned.

'I think it's time you did, don't you?' he asked tenderly.

Megan was delighted, until she realised that the gardener had arrived and was working on a flower-bed only a few yards away from them. Although his back was turned she knew that if she came after waiting so long, she wouldn't be able to help making a noise and then he'd know. 'Perhaps I'll wait a little longer,' she said tentatively.

'Nonsense,' replied Fabrizio. 'You know you need a climax. I hope you're not turning shy on me, not after all this time. If you're worried about the gardener, forget it. He's only an employee.'

'I was an employee once,' she reminded him.

'That was simply a way of getting you here,' he said with a laugh. 'This was what I wanted all along.'

He pushed the seat again and Megan felt the muscles of her belly rippling and her juices start to flow. She wriggled frantically on the seat, biting on her lower lip to stop herself from moaning. The next thing she knew, Fabrizio was crouching on the ground in front of her, his hands moving slowly up her legs, pushing her thighs apart until finally his fingers were moving through her pubic hair, tugging gently at it as he parted her outer sex lips. Then, as she began to quake with the delicious, hot, rising excitement, he moved his tongue around the entrance to her vagina, occasionally dipping it inside and then swirling it upwards around her frantic clitoris and she cried out as pleasure streaked through her like lightning.

Lifting his head Fabrizio smiled at her. 'You nearly came then didn't you?' Megan nodded. 'Say it,' he insisted. 'Say it loudly so that the gardener hears.'

'I can't,' she whispered.

'Then I'll leave,' said Fabrizio, starting to rise.

'No!' shouted Megan and the gardener turned his head a little before hastily getting back to his work.

'Say it then,' Fabrizio repeated.

'I want to come!' screamed Megan, all inhibitions gone as her body's desperate need drove her relentlessly towards release.

Smiling, Fabrizio bent his head and this time his mouth fastened over the hard little bud and he sucked, gently at first but then more strongly before moving his mouth lower, letting his nose slide over her clitoris while his tongue worked busily inside her.

The combination of sensations was incredible and her body responded with a shattering climax, so intense that the pleasure was mixed with pain. As the first contractions started to die away and Fabrizio fastened his mouth around her tender clitoris again she started to scream, because now he was forcing her to orgasm once more, and this time the streaks of pain were deeper, darker, but because of the way in which he'd trained her this only made the second orgasm even more satisfying.

'That's so good!' she shouted. 'Do it again, please.'

She saw that the gardener was watching them now, making no attempt to appear to be working, but she didn't care. All that mattered was this strange, perverse mixture of agony and ecstasy that Fabrizio had taught her to thrive on, and which her body craved every day. It was only after he'd forced three more orgasms from her that he finally lifted his head and, getting to his feet, unfastened her wrists before pulling her down onto the ground. Without any more preliminaries he unzipped himself and pushed roughly into her, his hands hard on her shoulders as she writhed beneath him on the soft grass, watching his face contort as his body finally spasmed too.

For a few seconds he lay on top of her, his mouth close to her ear as he whispered endearments in Italian, endearments that she still didn't understand but which she cherished because he said them so rarely. Then, with an abruptness that she'd grown to expect he withdrew from her and walked briskly back to the house, leaving her lying in an exhausted, dishevelled heap on the ground.

Struggling to her feet she straightened her clothing

and mustering all the courage that she could, she walked back to the house, passing within three feet of the gardener. He didn't look up, but she could feel his eyes watching her as soon as she was past. Once inside the house she hurried to take a shower, because she knew that in this sort of mood Fabrizio would probably want to take her again, possibly in the cellar where he played his most extreme games.

At nine o'clock that night Megan and Fabrizio finally sat down to dinner with Leonora and Franco. Megan, who'd been in the cellar with Fabrizio for nearly two hours, felt exhausted but happy. Looking round the table she realised how lucky she'd been to escape from what most people would consider a normal life and be given the chance to discover herself here in Sussex. Nick and the public library seemed a lifetime away and she felt proud of her new sexuality.

She was proud too of the astonishing freedom and pleasure that she'd gained through submission to Fabrizio's will. And he was so delighted with her responses to everything, that only a few days earlier he'd said impulsively that he didn't know how he'd live without her.

However, despite the wonderful day that they'd shared, Megan could see that Fabrizio looked less than happy. While the rest of them chattered away he was relatively quiet, only speaking when spoken to, and Megan sensed that his thoughts were elsewhere. She couldn't think what was the matter with him, but knew that it was important she found out. Even if he needed her as badly as she needed him, she was very aware that he'd trained her too well for her to be able to walk away, or exist without him should he tire of her.

'Do you think Fabrizio's all right?' she asked Leonora quietly, when they were drinking coffee after the meal.

Leonora shrugged. 'He seems fine to me.'

'He was very quiet at dinner.'

Leonora nodded. 'Of course. That's because he's getting bored.'

'Bored?' Megan hastily lowered her voice, afraid that Fabrizio might overhear. 'He can't be.'

For the first time ever, Leonora looked sympathetically at Megan. 'Why? Because the pair of you are having such a wonderful time? Because the four of us have done things that you'd never dreamt of before you came here? It isn't the same for him you know. He's done it all before, admittedly with other people, but nevertheless he's done it before. I think he suffers from a kind of Sexual Attention Deficit Disorder.'

Megan was horrified. 'If that's true, I don't know what to do,' she whispered.

'There's nothing you can do. Remember, Alessandra was in your position for a long time until he decided he needed a novelty, someone fresh. The next thing she knew, he no longer wanted her. Perhaps you should have thought about that a little more when she left, rather than being pleased to see the back of her.'

Megan didn't reply, because she knew that Leonora was speaking the truth. While in the cellar today Fabrizio had gone further than he'd ever gone before, and despite the pleasure that she'd gained there had been times when Megan had felt afraid, wondering how far down the road of debauchery Fabrizio was going to lead her. Now she had to think, and think fast, if she was to keep him and not end up like Alessandra.

Slipping into bed that night, curving her naked body round his back so that they were like two spoons, Megan slid her hand down Fabrizio's body and lightly caressed his penis. At first he didn't respond, but then as her fingers worked busily on him she felt him start to harden until she was able to sit astride him, feeling his long, hard cock slide deep inside her until it brushed the edge of her cervix. Staring down at him, but motionless, Megan decided that now was an ideal time to tell him the idea that had been hatched after her discussion with Leonora.

'You know,' she murmured huskily, 'I think the attic bedrooms need re-decorating.'

Fabrizio stared up at her in astonishment. 'Is this your idea of erotic talk?'

Megan began to rock backwards and forwards a little, stimulating herself, but not Fabrizio. 'You haven't let me finish.'

Fabrizio sighed. 'I'd have thought you knew by now that I'm not interested in domestic details.'

'You'll be interested in this one. I think we should advertise for an interior designer to work on the rooms. Someone quite young, without any ties. She could stay with us while she was doing the work.'

A light seemed to switch on behind Fabrizio's eyes and his full, sensual mouth curved upwards in a smile. 'Do you mean what I think you mean?'

'I mean that it's time for a new game,' said Megan.

'We don't want to get bored here, do we? It will be fun to have someone new join the four of us.'

Reaching upwards Fabrizio grasped Megan's breasts and began to massage them with his fingers, while at the same time thrusting upward with his hips so that Megan had to lean back in order to keep her balance. She could feel him expanding inside her as his excitement grew. 'Are you sure that's what you want, too?' he asked.

'I can't wait,' said Megan, with perfect honesty. 'I'd love to see someone as sexually inexperienced as I was when I came here being initiated by us all. It would be like watching myself, something that I never had the chance to do!'

'I knew you were special,' said Fabrizio, pulling Megan down and over to one side until the pair of them were lying next to each other, with him still deep inside her. Then, as his hands moved beneath her bottom and he pulled her back and forth on his massive erection, he began to talk about all the things that they'd do to the timid, innocent newcomer and how exciting it would be. As Megan listened her excitement grew until the pair of them climaxed together, before collapsing into each other's arms.

Fabrizio was quickly asleep, but Megan lay awake a little longer. She knew by the way that Fabrizio had responded to her suggestion that she'd done the right thing, and she'd been perfectly honest when she'd said that she was as excited as he was at the prospect. Now that she was more experienced she knew she would take pleasure from the initial resistance that the girl they finally chose would be sure to offer as they corrupted her, just as Megan herself had been corrupted.

A week later, a poised and calm Megan, no longer recognisable as the shy innocent who'd been interviewed by Fabrizio only a few months earlier, ushered a quiet, nondescript girl into the drawing room for an interview with Fabrizio. She was quite tall and slim, with light brown hair tied back off her face giving her the appearance of someone not long out of school. When the girl, whose name was Josephine, saw Fabrizio she looked astonished, taking a small step back in surprise.

Megan remembered how astonished she'd been in the same situation, because she'd been expecting an elderly member of the British aristocracy, and since she and Fabrizio had worded their advertisement carefully this girl had probably been expecting someone similar. As her innocent, soft brown eyes took in the dashing good looks of the handsome Italian, Josephine's cheeks flushed and Megan saw that the girl's hands were trembling slightly.

'I'll leave you two together now,' Megan said with a smile at the newcomer, and as she walked past her lover she gave him an almost imperceptible nod. Walking out of the room she realised that she was damp between her thighs. The sight of the girl, clearly a sexual innocent, and her reaction to Fabrizio had aroused her more than she'd expected and she could hardly wait for the moment when the four of them began to tutor the unsuspecting newcomer.

She pictured the ordeal that lay ahead of the girl, and although she felt a fleeting moment of pity for her, she knew that there was really no need because, like herself, she would experience the most incredible pleasure, pleasure that at the moment was far beyond her wildest imaginings. 'Yes,' said Megan aloud. 'I think Josephine will do very well indeed.'

Waiting for the bell to ring in the kitchen, which would be Fabrizio's signal for her to show the girl out, she wondered whether she should be nervous about letting a newcomer join them. After all, Alessandra had done the same thing, but Megan still felt totally secure. Alessandra hadn't been the one to initiate Megan joining the Balocchi household, and that was the difference.

Fabrizio now knew that Megan would always be looking for new things to excite them both, new ideas to give them pleasure, and that with her at his side he would never become bored. More importantly, neither would she.

As the interview went on and on, her right hand strayed between her thighs because her excitement was so great that she could no longer wait for Fabrizio to be free. Within a couple of minutes she'd brought herself to a shuddering climax and then, just as the last tremors died away, she heard the bell ring. With a flutter of anticipation she started to walk back to the library, knowing that another chapter in this house of decadence was about to begin.